Meredith Daneman was born in Tasmania and educated in Sydney, Australia. At sixteen she won a scholarship to the Royal Ballet School in London. She appeared at Covent Garden with the Royal Opera Ballet and was a founding member of the Australian Ballet. Her first novel, *A Chance to Sit Down*, was published in 1971; this was followed by *The Groundling* (1982) and *Francie and the Boys* (1988). She is currently working on a biography of Margot Fonteyn. She and her husband, the actor Paul Daneman, live in London and have two daughters.

D1392035

# The Favourite

## MEREDITH DANEMAN

*faber and faber*

LONDON · BOSTON

First published in 1993
by Faber and Faber Limited
3 Queen Square London WC1N 3AU
Open market paperback edition first published in 1994
This paperback edition first published in 1994

Printed in England by Clays Ltd, St Ives Plc.

The lines from the songs on pages 46–7 are quoted by
permission of Williamson Music: 'What's the use of
Wond'rin' from *Carousel*, lyrics by Oscar Hammerstein II,
music by Richard Rogers, copyright © Williamson Music,
1945; 'Something Wonderful' from *The King and I*, lyrics by
Oscar Hammerstein II, music by Richard Rogers, copyright
© Richard Rogers and Oscar Hammerstein II, 1951.

A CIP record for this book is
available from the British Library

ISBN 0–571–17153–2

2 4 6 8 10 9 7 5 3 1

To Paul

# The Favourite

There are only two kinds of mother, fussy or neglectful, take your pick. As a mother myself I have fussed incurably: don't be long, have you eaten, where's your coat. But my standard of motherhood has always been neglect. A real mother, my own mother, the mother I still yearn to please long after she's dead, doesn't look up, doesn't check if I'm warm enough, lets me go hungry out into the night without a curfew. It's not that she doesn't love me. She notices some things, not to do with my welfare: if I'm looking excited, whether or not I'm wearing lipstick. Your hair looks nice dear, she says, where are you going? And the result is I'm hardly ever going anywhere, I'd rather stay home with her, waiting for my father. He's always storming off somewhere without his coat or a proper meal inside him and never coming back. He's the type of man you can rely on to go on leaving you. She's worn herself out worrying what's become of him; that's why she can't be bothered any more to worry about me. I don't mind: I consider her carelessness a compliment. She's not so complimentary to my sisters because they're older and younger than I am: her eldest, in whom she's invested all her ideals, and her baby, to whom she clings as her last hope. But I'm free, I'm in the middle, I've slipped through the suffocating net of her protection. At the age of ten I already know things I shouldn't. She hardly treats me like a child at all. She can't afford to: she needs me for a most un-childlike purpose. Whenever my father threatens to leave home, I'm the one who's supposed to make him stay.

Why are you going? I ask him, but we both know he can't answer. He can't bring me up to believe that sex is the reason that everyone does everything in the end.

We're on the ferry, sailing towards the city. I'm riding with him, seeing what it's like to be setting out with a suitcase packed with clean white shirts badly ironed by my mother. But when we get to town he'll be getting off, and I'll be taking the round trip home again on my own.

We're on the outside deck leaning over the rail; being so long, his legs are stretched out at an angle behind him to trip up passers-by. He doffs his hat politely to them as they fall past. My father behaves adorably to strangers. It's only people he knows that he deigns to treat badly.

The glare of the sun on the water is making me screw up my eyes. It's a hot day, and out here on the harbour there's a high cool wind. The perfection of the weather is beginning to get seriously oppressive. I'm carrying a letter from my mother which I'm supposed to give him, although I know that nothing written is ever going to stop him now. But I'm here on her behalf, so I hand it over, true to her instructions if despairing of her methods; he puts it in his pocket to read later.

Read it now, I say, with my unanswerable child's authority, and he can't be a coward in front of me, he takes the letter out of its envelope, turns his back to the rail and studies the pages diligently, albeit without his glasses. My mother's a talented writer, even the notes she dashes off to the milkman are moving; my father fell in love with her on paper. But now her best efforts can't reach him, the pages flutter helplessly in his hand, the wind has more use for them than he does, and already I'm wishing they would blow away and hit the water face-down; I want my mother's words to run and go soggy and sink, rather than be looked at so drily for a moment longer.

You'll be better off without me, he says finally, folding the letter and putting it back in his pocket, and that's when I start to cry and shake my head violently, even though we're outside, in a public place, with people staring.

He thinks, stupid man, that I'm upset for myself; he says, You know, don't you, that you're the only one I really care about; if it weren't for you I wouldn't care what happened to me at all. And I believe him, although he's doubtless said such things to other women. I know from the look on his face that what he says is true. I look away quickly, his love for me strikes me as terrible, disloyal to my mother, insulting to my sisters; I think I'd even prefer it if he told me he loved his mistress. I stare down at water churning up in our wake as the ferry slows down towards the quay, praying he won't say it, but he does.

If you're too unhappy, he says, later on you can come and live with me. And then the real unhappiness starts, the insupportable thought of being without my mother, her sad laugh, the softness of her look. I'm ten, but I can't understand how a man of forty can't see that I *am* my mother: it's me he's really leaving when he leaves her, it's she whom he really loves when he says he loves me.

I couldn't, I say, and immediately it seems to be the cruellest thing that any of us has said: my unkindness seems to bow him down, to strike at his tallness, at the jaunty angle of his hat.

We don't say any more because of the noise of the engines shuddering into neutral, the crash of gang planks as the ferry ties up to the wharf. So that when he walks away from me, despite the suitcase he's carrying, the impression is that I'm rejecting him, sending him away. The sight of his newly stooped back makes me call after him – I will come, I will – but he doesn't hear me, or pretends not to, afraid perhaps that I'll follow him; and then where would he take me? Where's he going anyway? To his office, some woman's place? Don't ask. Once safely ashore with several feet of choppy water between us, I'm convinced he'll turn around, and wave, but he doesn't, it's as though he's already not thinking of me; he joins the crowd walking towards the ticket barrier, his step purposeful, his shoulders square once more. And then at the last moment he turns, and in that sweet chivalrous gesture he usually reserves for mere acquaintances or lucky strangers, he raises his hat to me, and is gone. And that is who I cry for in the night, that is who I believe every

6

time is never coming back: not the man who leaned on the rail beside me, seeming to make the boat list with the dangerous weight of his sentiment, but that gallant, affable figure in the distance, his hat raised in half feigned yet delighted recognition.

I'm five and I'm running with a small leather case in my hand. I've found it, and I like it, it's exactly the right scale for me: a miniature suitcase for a miniature person, and I run with it through the house from one room to another; there are long passages and many stairs, a person with luggage can travel far. My father sees me coming and shouts, Where are you going with *that*? and there's something in his voice that frightens and excites me; I have to find my mother before he can take it away from me, I have to get the suitcase to *her*. She appears as she always does at the sound of his raised voice, and at the sight of her I trip because my eyes are, as always, immediately tied to her face, watching for the gentleness of her favour. And as I fall, the case flies from my hand and lands neatly at her feet, opening magically on impact and shedding its fateful contents all over her shoes: love letters, scores of them, written to my father, in a hand she's never seen before in her life.

And years later, when she recounted the anecdote, which she often did, animated, as by nothing else in her old age, by the memory of my father's infidelities, she would say in a tone of admiring collusion, as though I had been her agent, her ally, Trust *you* to be the one to let the cat out of the bag. I could always rely on you to be in at the kill. Where could you have found that beastly little case? How did you know what was in it? Why did you bring it to me?

And I didn't know, couldn't tell her, only really remembered the incident in her terms because I had been told of it so graphically; had it muddled in my memory anyway with another incident in which I also ran through the house, having veered too close to the electric heater and set my pinafore alight. I ran on that occasion, calling out in a small, oddly ineffectual voice that no one but she could have heard, holding out the smoking apron in front of me by the skirt as though it were an offering, a present. I bore everything to her in those days, love letters, burning pinnies, like a cat bringing dead birds to its horrified owner; I was fired with the purpose of finding her, and dragging my father's treasures to her feet.

Who's this? says my elder daughter, Mary, flashing one of my husband's newspaper cartoons too close to my face.

It's a new character of Daddy's, I tell her. Some colleague of Harry's, I think, at the office.

No, I mean who is she *really*? says Mary; and she's right, it must be someone. My husband's (Frank's) drawings are always of real people. I am one of his characters, so is Mary and so is her baby sister, Edith, although she's been translated, for the sake of equity, into a boy. Together with Frank's impressions of himself as the husband, Harry, we make up a funny family called The Blades for people to laugh at weekly on a Sunday. I myself have been through many a metamorphosis in his drawings, but at the moment I'm an ex-flower-child in a droopy cardigan who lugs a baby about on her ever-broadening hip. The cartoon Mary is a frowning seven-year-old with reformist tendencies who demands to know the answer to everything.

Is she going to be in it every week, says the real Mary, frowning, or is it just this once?

I don't know, I say with a shrug. Ask your father. But

later I pick up the folded-back newspaper and hold it at a decent distance from my eyes.

It's not one of Frank's better drawn characters. It's my opinion, my guess, that it doesn't come from life. He's dreamt this woman up. It's not that she's so beautiful: she's older than I am by the look of her, and what he's got her saying isn't particularly riveting. What's wrong is there's nothing wrong with her. All his characters have some flaw, some adorable asymmetry of line, something unfinished or overdone in their execution. But this woman is perfect. She's not funny. I can't see the point of having her in the story. I want to say to him, Frank, who is this person? I really think you ought to phase her out. But something (Mary) alerts me to the danger of mentioning her. It's to do with my believing she comes from his imagination. You can't say to someone you love, I think your fantasy is a bit on the mundane side – perhaps you ought to stick to the exotica of everyday life.

But a day or two later I do mention it. I'm not very honourable when it comes to matters of art. Who *is* this woman? I say. What on earth is she wearing? Exactly what colour is her hair supposed to be? Not, actually, the questions I was planning to ask at all.

How do *I* know? he says, squinting. It's in black and white. Mary's always colouring in my cartoons – ask her.

Mary doesn't think much of this character, I say, not altogether truthfully. She wants to know if she's going to be a regular feature.

Frank shrugs: how does *he* know? He's incapable of

telling what will happen next without a pencil in his hand.

I take his tip about the colouring in, but I don't ask Mary. I borrow her Derwent pencils while she's at school and have a go myself. Edith, the baby, watches me: she's too young to tell, but even in front of her I feel furtive and inhibited. Married to a proper artist, it's years since I've attempted to draw so much as a stick man. The pencils delight me with their soft, graduated colours lined up in their graduated rows. I'm so busy sharpening them and re-organizing them in sequence that I almost forget my purpose. Flesh is the colour most nearly worn down to the stub – so many legs and arms and necks and faces to fill in. I fill in the flesh I know first. The daughter, the baby, the husband and, after a second sharpening session, the wife. I wonder if this new character warrants any further wearing away of Mary's most coveted colour. I decide not, and plump for a less delicate tint, lightly applied. After all, the woman may go once a week to a sun-bed. I give her a blue jumper to set off her tan and then tackle the problem of her hair. I'm torn between brassy and mouse and don't know how to achieve either. By now the margin at the edge of the newspaper is striped with test scribbles of carrot and corn. In the end the hair stays plain. It's time for me to pick up Mary from school. But the strange thing is, I feel the need to destroy my handiwork. I don't want Frank or Mary to come across it. I tear the half page cartoon into little pieces. Then I screw up the rest of the page in case they notice it's been torn out. Finally I put the whole newspaper into a plastic bag in case anyone notices the page is missing, and take it with me in the car on the drive to school. At the end of the lane I stop and dump the bag in somebody else's skip. Edith watches me from her car seat with a censorious gaze. Probably when she learns to speak it'll be the first thing she mentions. Edith is bald: the colour of *her* hair is a mystery to me as well. I have no idea as yet of its barley-field variegations, its smell, its swinging straightness, the way it will cling and part at the back of her neck as she leans forward, drawing, like her father, dragging images to consciousness, bringing the future to meet us, with her tongue pressed firmly into her cheek.

# 4

Where trouble is, there am I, running towards it. This time I'm sprinting across the school playground while taken up with something diverting over my right shoulder. I go smack into a metal goal post and drop rather dramatically to my knees. Teachers and pupils come running. Blood oozes painlessly out of my temple above my left eyebrow. Just as I'm being led off to the sick bay, the headmistress, Mrs Witherby, intervenes. I'm to go with her, apparently, to her office.

My heart, already bumping from the incident, thuds faster. There's obviously some school rule against knocking yourself senseless in the playground. I try to convey with my wobbly walk that I'm not in the mood to write a hundred lines. She guides me through her office to another small room beyond, with an old-fashioned day bed propped against one wall. So snoozing is what she gets up to while we slave away at multiplication.

Lie down, dear, she says, I'll be back in a minute. And so she is, with a bowl of warm water and a wad of cotton wool.

There's something about your headmistress tending

to you that doesn't feel quite right. Not that Mrs Witherby is a particularly forbidding woman. Though known as The Widow, she's actually quite young and personable, and there's something smooth and sensitive about her face that I would like, were it not my natural schoolgirl instinct to hate her. As it is, the gentleness of her hand on my forehead and the strangely searching way she looks into my face make me long to be sent on my way with a detention. But I'm detained here. She's sent off to the staff room for a cup of tea with extra sugar. When I sit up to drink it I feel a bit woozy and have to lie down again. Mrs Witherby's large eyes lose focus, so profound is her anxiety. I must go and make a phone call, she says.

She closes the door between the two rooms, and I hear her voice, lowered, on the telephone. For the first time I'm starting to feel a bit alarmed about my condition. Am I going to die? If so, I'd rather do it somewhere other than here. I can't work out why her concern for my welfare is so personal. Can the school be sued for positioning goal posts in the paths of hurrying children?

I've rung your father, she says, coming back into the room.

My father? I cry, sitting up in a panic, forgetting her authority in the face of a higher one. You shouldn't have bothered *him*. He hates to be rung at the office. Sometimes he's not even there. Why didn't you ring my mother? I'm perfectly all right anyway.

No you're not, says Mrs Witherby, looking a little flustered, but charmed for some reason by my lack of a proper respect. Your father's business number was the first to hand. I thought he would probably have a car and could pick you up.

There's no denying her logic, but I say defiantly, My mother could've easily come on the tram. It's too difficult for my father. He's got too much responsibility to be able to get away.

A curious triumph coarsens Mrs Witherby's fine features. He'll be here in twenty minutes, she says quietly. So just lie back and relax.

Actually it takes him half an hour. The Widow makes constructive use of the time. She sits by my bedside, asking me personal questions. I can't see what the sort of house we live in, and what my mother does with herself all day, and what we do as a family at weekends can possibly have to do with my academic progress. But she seems to find it a matter of headmistressly concern. It must be the bang on the head, but I find I'm unduly talkative. Her loss of propriety in asking and her flushed, slightly wincing attention to my answers makes me reach for the kind of detail that is not exactly bound by accuracy.

Well, I say, it varies. We often *mean* to go to church. Often we get all ready to go, and then something happens to stop us. (Like my father calling on the Lord to witness that my mother hasn't done the washing-up.)

Do your parents agree, Rosalind? Ideologically, I mean?

(No, Mrs Witherby, they do not. Ideologically or otherwise.)

Yes, I think so, I say. On the whole. Maybe my father is more religious than my mother. Or at least he comes from a more religious background. Although he says he's the black sheep of the family.

A smile takes Mrs Witherby's lips by surprise. She tries to frown it away. Does he read to you from the Bible? she asks soberly. She runs a church school, after all.

He tells us stories, I answer. Out of his head. His favourite is the Prodigal Son.

Again the daft smile overtakes her. And your mother, she says, as though to punish herself, what's her favourite?

Oh, nothing from the *Bible*, I say scornfully. She prefers the plots of things she's seen in the theatre. Madame Butterfly or stuff by Noël Coward. Or sometimes she tells us the stories of plays she's written herself. My mother would be a brilliant writer, you see, if she didn't have to look after all of us.

Mrs W's smile is no longer giving her trouble. A darker, less charitable mood is upon her. Just how well *does* she look after you, she is about to ask, when my father arrives with an arpeggio of knocks at the outer door.

She closes the door between us to let him in. She intercepts a father hurrying to his injured child: between her and me it is suddenly out and out war. To hear his voice and have her keep him from me causes my head, where the swelling is, to throb unendurably. Through a haze of pain I think I hear him calling her Angela. Daddy! I call out before she can call him Jim.

He's through the door as I speak: it's no contest really. How tall he is, how white and fierce his face. Mrs Witherby follows, looking small and twittery in his shadow. I can hardly connect her any more with the woman who conducts prayers in assembly.

I don't understand, she's saying. She was feeling all right until you arrived. We were having a good talk, weren't we, Rosalind. I took particular care of her, as you can imagine. Look – the cut was too small to consider stitches. She's only going to have a nasty bruise.

I cry uncontrollably lest she dare touch me. I can't bear her now I know her name is Angela. Despite his bad back (he suffers from crippling sciatica), my father picks me up. He sweeps me up into his arms, muttering about doctors and concussion, and a week later my sisters and I leave the school. We're taken away from our sedate ladies' college and sent to the rough state school round the corner where I'm likely to run into a few worse things than goal posts. My father no longer believes in private education. He's had an ideological change of heart.

## 5

I know about other women. I've been another woman myself. When I first met Frank he was married, and while his wife was away I used to sleep in her bed, in the ten-year-old dent in her mattress.

I worry about the sheets. Not whether he's changed them before I've come so much as whether he'll change them afterwards. Matters of laundry don't usually come top of my list. Why should they? I'm only eighteen; there's nothing of the housewife in my blood. It's my blood that may get on the sheets. Not that I'm a virgin or anything: it's just that his wife's plans don't take my menstrual cycle into account. Frank doesn't care. Things like blood are a bonus with him, an unexpected splash of colour. Just think how safe we are, he says.

I don't feel safe at all. What if she comes home and finds us? But he says she won't, and I'm afraid he speaks from experience. Other other women have slept in this bed before me. I'm not entirely encouraged by his confidence: I keep a look-out over his shoulder in case we don't hear her key in the lock, what with all the noise we're making. In a sense she's looming at the foot of the bed all the time. Does her ghost add to our excitement? I have no point of comparison. I'm so used to slipping in and out of the back door of his life that I don't know how it would feel to be respectable.

For all my worldly ways, this is the first whole night I've spent in bed with anyone. I'm not sure I like it. Not him, you understand – I love *him*. But the double dark, the constricted space, the shared unconsciousness. How can I give myself up to that as though it were natural? It's natural to him: he falls asleep like a child. Which is ironic, since he's old enough to be my father. My own childishness takes me differently: I'm wide-eyed, perverse, over-excited. I want to shake him awake, but the authority of his quiet, even breathing awes and slightly hurts me – how can he cut off from me like that? Will he know which one I am, when he wakes up? His head on the pillow has an heroically backward tilt, his insensibility strikes me as courageous. Coward-ice besets me all night. By dawn I'm completely exhaus-ted. But he does know who I am when he stirs. Roz, he says, Rosa, my Rose.

I make love with more valour in the daylight. It's morning, and she hasn't come after all. It *is* better with-out her shadow standing over us. Now I could sleep, now I could lie here all day. But it's his turn to be ner-vous: the cleaner might arrive at any moment. I'm full of bravado in the face of his discomfort – hard to rouse, easy to offend, must have a bath. He brings me break-fast in bed to hurry and placate me. Toast and marma-lade and tea. It's the most unswallowable meal I've ever tasted. The tea is too strong and too milky, he's put sugar in it without asking. Is there something wrong with the bread knife that he's cut the bread so coarsely?

The marmalade, piled on thickly, is full of bitter chunks. Thank you, I say, how sweet of you, how delicious; and his pleasure in pleasing me plays havoc with his will-power. Stay, he says. What the hell, let me make you some more. Your cleaner is coming, I remind him. You know I must go.

So I went, not just home, but as far away as possible. I left this country I'd escaped to and went back to my family in Australia: it was the fashion, in those days, to behave well. But I have to admit that I wrote. Love letters, scores of them, enough to fill a small leather suitcase. I suppose I must have hoped they would fall out one day at his wife's feet.

My father hangs from a tree. The branch he's swinging on bends and creaks under his weight and his feet are a few inches from the fast-flowing water which we've been told we mustn't swim in because of sharks. He's disturbed a nest of insects in the tree. Bees or hornets or worse swarm round his head and hands. We can't get the boat back in reach of him because of underwater snags. It was trying to push us off the snags that made him grab hold of the tree in the first place. In his effort to kick us free, he's left himself dangling there. Now the choice is not whether to die but which way: will it be the bees or the sharks that get him? Jump! shouts my elder sister. Hang on! cries my younger. For myself the most urgent thing seems to be to stop him making that terrible howling noise, which I realize to my horror is laughter. He's helpless, the whole tree is shaking, he's going to die of a slapstick joke. Stop it, Daddy, I shout, but it's too late: the bough breaks and down he comes, feet first into the dark, murky river. He goes right under and is gone for some time, shedding wasps perhaps, or unhooking his clothing from some snag (I don't like to think it was to frighten us), so that when he erupts to the surface, and swims towards us with a wild, wind-mill, shark-defying style, and then hauls himself, unaided, into the boat, the sheer physical sense of him is such that it is indeed as though he's come back from the dead, or is himself a monster from the deep.

The next time he nearly dies I think he's joking. But he's not, he's choking. We're eating bloody steak, cooked over a camp fire. My sisters aren't here this time to offer advice or hysteria: it isn't really an outing for children. I'm standing in for my mother because she doesn't like the people we've come with – two business friends of my father's and their wives, and the inevitable spare woman with rolling eyes. They're what my mother calls too social for her, and I must say they do drink rather a lot. The women have husky voices, skinny figures and ageing skin and the men thump each other on the back a lot, a gesture that proves surprisingly ineffective when my father gets the bit of steak stuck. One minute he's talking with his mouth full and laughing his yelping laugh, and the next he's going blue in the face.

Stop it Daddy, I say, you know it's not funny. But he starts to make an even more comical sound. A terrible, unmanly, high-pitched rhythmical whine. Hold him upside down, shouts someone who used to be a nurse, it's what you do with babies; but of course there's no one tall enough or strong enough to up-end my six foot four inch father and swing him unceremoniously by his ankles. I've run a little way off now and am down on the ground with my face buried in the charred and ant-ridden earth. I'm praying, I suppose, although all I say

23

is, Please. Above all I want the terrible whining noise to stop. But I have to bear it as proof that he's still alive.

When at last there's silence, I can't look up. I've never seen a dead person before. But one of the husbands comes over and helps me to my feet. It's all right dear, he says, your father's got his breath back now.

And sure enough he's still with us, surrounded by solicitous women. The spare one, the one who used to be a nurse, has had the presence of mind to put her fingers down his throat. The thought of her nicotine pads in intimate contact with his epiglottis has an emetic effect on me as well, but I go over, as I'm expected to, and stand beside her. Once again, my father in his resurrected state frightens me slightly. Although he's on his knees on the grass, the power of new life seems to leap in him. He looks at me with eyes that might never have seen me again. I can't return his look in front of these people. In any case, the spare woman is rolling her eyes and demanding her dues. She leans against him on the way back in the car. Her hair is not naturally fair. My father owes his life to a woman who is not my mother, and for a moment I wish he were dead.

There were two men in my life before I went to England and met Frank. It would be neat to say I was in love with the one I didn't sleep with and slept with the one I didn't love, but it wouldn't be true. I didn't love either of them. I knew this with the clear judgement of youth which can distinguish, where maturity cannot, the difference between sentiment and desire. But I did desire the one I resisted, more than the one to whom I succumbed. These things are a matter of chronology; it's the first time that counts.

He was an Englishman called Alfred. Not Alf, or Fred, but Alfred: he was a stickler for full names. Not that he called me by my proper name, Rosalind. He wanted to, he thought it would give him special status with me, but I wouldn't let him, wouldn't answer to it, it reminded me of teachers or my father when he was angry. I made him call me Ro, like my friends did at school. It's important what he called me because he used my name unnaturally often, like a doctor, as though the reassuring repetition of a known word would make what he was doing to me seem less sinister. 'Ro,' he would plead against my ear, 'Ro,' incidentally turning my no, no into a foolish rhyme which I would have to give up eventually for aesthetic reasons. Perhaps he was really trying to remind himself who I was. Considering where we usually were when he had his hand up my skirt, it's surprising that he didn't call me Doris.

We went to the pictures quite often: there wasn't really anywhere else to go. Always to matinées – he had to go to work at night. I don't know whether he liked Doris Day, or imagined that I did, which I didn't. But she seemed to make it her business to be up there on the screen, her eyes widening comically as his hand found its way through the maze of roped petticoats, played little snapping games in passing with my suspenders, and then hovered around the edges of my knicker elastic until her lips duly parted in that wide, candid, dauntless, all-conquering smile. Bright in the dark, she covered for us, created a diversion, convinced us with her crisply buttoned collars and stiffly sprayed hair that nothing untoward could possibly be happening under the folds of a carefully draped sports jacket in the second row from the back.

We stared straight ahead, but I can see him now beside me, his white, half submerged shirtsleeves ghostly in the gloom. His hair, brushed back from his face in a quiff, grows low on his forehead: my mother says a low hairline is a sign of inferior intelligence, but he seems knowing enough, and a genius with his fingers. His profile is immobile, unruffled, at odds with the seething activity going on under the sports jacket. I am thrilled by this outward show of innocence and stillness: duplicity, for a schoolgirl, is a prerequisite of excitement. He is glamorous enough in the half-dark, although in fact it hardly matters what he looks like, any more than it matters which tall dark and handsome leading man is laying siege to the mythic maidenhood of the redoubtable Miss Day. What we are all hanging on is her reaction, how she will take it, whether she will scream or clamp her thighs together or call the police. Because I can have him clapped in gaol for this – I am fifteen and he is thirty; such power over men will never be mine again. But I just sit there, powerless, letting him, although letting him is all I do; I don't writhe about or squirm against his hand or offer any reciprocal favours, that's not what he wants, that would come as a shock to him, put him off probably: all he wants from me is my passive acquiescence.

This is how it feels then, and what seems to be making my breathing come so strangely is his remoteness, my delinquency, these trite, unrelated visions. Fatal associations, all. There is a potent note in the actress's voice, a hoarseness, a sudden catch in her laughter that might redeem us both. I'm faint with arousal but it comes to nothing: I'm ignorant in such matters and for all I know so is he; in any case it isn't part of his plan to assuage my desire but to raise it to the same ruthless pitch as his own. As Rock, is it, or Cary draws Doris into the final obligatory clinch, he takes his fingers away abruptly and holds them, for the length of a screen kiss, over my mouth and nose. And so overcome am I by the fumes from my own body, that for a moment I think I love him.

I love you, I mouth against his hand, and he is made absurdly happy, not by what he's divined I've said, but

27

by the evidence that I'm weakening, he's breaking down my resistance and soon I will be bound to give in.

Not so. Up on the screen the leather-skinned love-goddess breaks briskly from the embrace. Clearing her throat, she smooths out her skirt and sets her jaw in renewed and invigorated virtue. He will wear me down, win me round, convince me beyond recall of the illogicality, indeed the immorality of my position. But his efforts will be for somebody else. The pattern is set between us: for him I am the jam jar you try and try to open and finally set aside in frustration. And then some other sod picks it up idly and the lid comes off in one go.

# 8

Frank's brilliance as a cartoonist is that he is able to dramatize happiness. The Blades are a happy family. And family happiness, as Tolstoy famously pointed out, is undifferentiated. It does not come in scenes. It is a sweet, sprawling boredom that goes on year after year after year after year after year. Until one day . . .

We're so used to the atmosphere between us that we hardly notice it, except in the looks of outsiders who sit sometimes at our breakfast table, as we pick holes in each other's arguments and crumbs off each other's faces, their toast suddenly sticking in their throats at the pang of not being us. But Frank can turn perpetuity into a moment. He can draw neat rectangles round our formless gestures and contain the hot air of our talk in little balloons. And we don't mind being edited. We're happy to be the well from which his humour springs. We're used to the facts of our lives being spread all over the Sunday papers. What we like less are his protective efforts to disguise us. *That's* not what I'd say, says Mary, frowning over the proofs. And what have you given me plaits for when you know I'd never wear them? She is scandalized most by his turning her newborn sister, Edith, into a boy. To her mind he's harbouring a shameful preference for a son, not to mention secret longings for a train set. Whereas in fact the poor man is only trying *not* to betray the utter lopsidedness of his inclination: the shameless pleasure and pride he takes in being hag-ridden. And young Eddy turns out to have a pretty effeminate way with him on paper. So, to please us, Frank confines his comic invention to the truth. Until of course the day comes when the only way to keep pleasing us is with lies.

## 9

The game was this. You took off your knickers and climbed into the back seat of Annabel Rider's father's Buick. You slid over to the front passenger seat on to the lap of a girl who lifted up your skirt (little girls always wore dresses) and spanked you, once, on the bare bottom. Then you pulled down your skirt and clambered over the gearbox, past the steering wheel, out of the driver's door. The game took place during beautiful outdoor weather in the petrol-reeking confines of a sunless garage and was played in strict rotation and at high speed – the speed and the rotation were everything: pushing for your turn, scrambling over the leather upholstery, leaping out of the way of the person following behind. The slap was perfunctory and not very forcibly administered: we were masochists, not sadists, to a girl. In all charity I must have had my go as spanker, but I have no memory of bodies thudding on to my lap. Only of being in the fray, with my skirt now up, now down, and the sense of someone's mother about to find us.

As a mother myself, stumbling across the memory of it now, what scandalizes me about the game is its innocence. Its extraordinary, repetitive, boring want of invention. Was that all we could think of to do? And in a car, of all spiritless places? And given the poverty of our six-year-old imaginations, what real-life experience were we drawing on? How many of our fathers would pull down their female children's pants in the name of chastisement? Not Annabel Rider's, or Carolyn Croft's, surely. Only mine. Only mine. It occurs to me in shame that the idea of the game must have come from me.

He did it once to my younger sister in the street. What struck you about my father, apart from his hand, was the extraordinary technical proficiency of his actions: one minute she was lagging behind, or whining, or spilling her ice-cream down her front, or whatever she was doing to incur his white-faced wrath, and the next she was suspended horizontally under his arm, with her knickers caught round her knees, and he was dealing brisk blows to her sun-lit bottom.

The pain I felt was not really for my sister. Her lagging and whining and messy way with ice-cream irritated me as well, and her white, unwriggling bum looked plumply impervious to his spread-palmed, reddened hand. What was more, she wailed without inhibition, and I would have had him hit her harder to shut her up. No, it was for him that I was dying, that he could do this in the open: this dreadful, disgracing, preposterously ribald thing.

And yet no one crossed the street to say don't do that. Perhaps they thought him justified: his child was his child. Or perhaps they had the compassion to leave us alone. Our father was our father.

He certainly did seem to have more right than my aunt, his sister, who when she came to stay with us went in for the same routine, on even more obscure provocation, and with a harsher, redder hand. I screamed at her as I would never have dared scream at my father, and reared my bared behind vulgarly close to her face. But in fact my anger was a rush of buoyant confidence to discover that he was not the only one: it was a family not a fatherly aberration, a prurient Victorian ritual that had been handed down impersonally, not personally dreamed up. Was it my grandfather or my grandmother who had done it to him? I wanted to know the lineage of my hatred. But they were both dead, and all that their faces expressed in old albums was the Fear of God (that strange, still, stern, sepia half-smile), which they had put so fatally into my father, and he with his hand to my backside planned to put into me. For these spankings had a religious connotation: the ghastly solemnity of a duty being painfully carried out. There was a piety to the pulling down of the pants that disgusted me more than the violence, which was, in fact, marginal: it did not hurt, much. In punishing us, my father was, above all, keeping his word. He always warned us. Despite the fierce suddenness with which he grabbed my sister in the street, it was unthinkable that he wouldn't have issued some threat, If you dare do that again . . . and of course you did. Our mother, who could lash out quite viciously, only ever did so in hot blood, and her passing blows, though stinging, were as forgettable as they were unpremeditated. But with my father there was always a strange, paralysed, dream time, the time between: If your room isn't tidy by the time I come home . . . and the dread sound of his returning tread on the stairs. And somehow, from the moment of the warning, obedience was impossible: some deep, childish honour bound you to the punishment; the shame of it spread backward and branded you in advance. For it was shame my father dealt in – the pink of your buttocks would be pallid compared with the dark rush of crimson to the cheeks of your face.

You knew what was to come and yet you just sat there. The scattered toys and clothes stared back at you from the floor. There was nothing to be done, no way to begin. The clothes and the toys were too many, the cupboards already full. A strange inertia possessed you, unusual in an active, healthy child; it was as though your ankles were already bound by the soft, elastic drag of your lowered knickers. Chaos was everywhere, in your head, all over the floor. Order was inconceivable. It belonged in some way to your father, and the only way back to it was through the fire of his terrible anger. The only thing to do was to wait. Hum a little tune, read a book, until the time passed. Hope that although the room could not be tidied, he might be detained, caught up by some grand complication in the outside world.

Our mother would come in and try to hurry things along. Do tidy up, darling, she would say. Your father will be back any minute. She would even do a bit herself, to help you. But she had no talent for it. Untidiness, the great crime of our childhood, was the thing we had inherited, in our genes, from her. Even as she opened the cupboard doors, the spirit failed her. She really had no earthly idea how to do it. More things fell out than she managed to stuff away. Don't bother,

34

Mum, you'd say, I'll do it; and she'd sigh and believe you. There was an innocence about our mother in the face of mundane life. Household objects had an autonomy that she couldn't control. Whole rooms would fill up with kept newspapers, from which she planned to cut out articles about film stars. Oh, she would say, oh dear, this door won't shut. One door that often wouldn't shut was the door of the fridge. Forever undefrosted, the ice compartment grew silently in the night. The food won't fit in, she'd say. This fridge seems to have got smaller. Sometimes the whole house got smaller, and we had to move. We'd moved four times before I was seven; and still the creeping detritus encroached from the walls. She spent the time idling that she should have spent tidying. But while she stood in your room, idly smiling, your father was the one who was mad.

When he came home she would plead for me, but he'd order her away. This is between me and Rosalind, he'd say, although it was not: it was between him and the part of me that was most invincibly on her side. I was glad when she left the room. I did not want her to see what he did, any more than I wanted any well-meaning stranger to cross the street and intervene. My father's fury was unleashed, and must have its way. And really, once it all began, my blood would pound so blackly and my thoughts would come so thickly that I hardly knew anything, until the final moment, the moment upon which he always insisted, when with my clothing adjusted I would sit on his lap and be forgiven. Or forgive him. I forget which way round it was meant to be. Either way, the mawkish inference was that we were still friends. *He* may have been. I was not. I am not now, and cannot ever be.

Oh, I know it was not so dreadful, what he did. There are fathers one hears of these days who do worse things. Who take out their unexpected cocks and shove them up their little girls' tender anuses. And these children's rooms, if they have them, are probably quite orderly. My father did not rape me. He didn't even beat me black and blue. It was not actually my body he had designs on: such was the lunacy of his upbringing that he thought through the purging of my flesh to cow my spirit. But children learn what they learn. And perhaps our understanding is our own. I passed on what he taught me to my friends as erotic adventure. And even as their shrieks gratified my ears, the fear of him was damp between my legs, and stronger in my nostrils than the smell of petrol.

## 10

My daughter Mary's game, at the age of six, is to hit herself. She gallops through the beechwoods whacking herself intermittently with a branch. She is, though you might not immediately twig it, a horse; she has the hard hat and the jodhpurs to prove it. Watch! she cries bossily, leaping a self-imposed two-inch high hurdle, mythic to herself, half animal, half rider.

Frank and I watch with some embarrassment. Her fantasy, all too common in posh little girls, is not one we can share. We don't dream of hot flanks squeezed between our thighs, or mucking out. We are city folk, from Sydney and London, native to the fumes of carbon monoxide. Yet it was our fantasy to bring her here to the country, to surround her with all these acres and expose her to the reactionary forces of nature. At first she used to miss our city square. Let's go to the park, she'd say, standing in the middle of the park we'd bought her. But now she likes it. She prefers the wormy earth to pale sandpits. She wants to see things grow, including my stomach. It's upon her insistence that I'm pregnant with unborn Edith: she'd have the baby for me, if it were physically possible. According to her teacher, the nearer the time comes for me to go into labour the less she can concentrate at school. She's susceptible to my fears, though she doesn't know what they are. I'm frightened this proxy child of hers will be nothing to me. Mary is my child, and I'm quite satisfied. Her jokes are the best I've ever heard, and at six she has a reading age of thirty-five. Her face is exactly the one Frank and I dreamed into being; we recognize its quaint fury, its swimming-eyed brightness. Why would I choose to forsake her face for another? But she needs people to put in this park of hers, so I do it for her, my reader, my intrepid rider.

The appointed day passes, and nothing happens. They put my feet in stirrups and start me off, of all disgusting expressions. I started of my own accord with Mary. It's not necessary to do this, I say to the doctor, who does the deed dressed in a sari, and my fear of her steel instrument is so primitive I think it's because I'm white that she won't listen. Someone gives me an enema too late. You're doing this the wrong way round, I explain, but she goes on pumping. Everything's pouring out of me at once. In fact I have to peer down the lavatory to make sure the baby hasn't been lost in the rush. But it's left high and dry in that first, faint, distant intimation of pain. You stiffen to it like an animal, nose raised to the scent, the heat, not just of life but of mortality: the rattle in your throat will sound the same. It isn't the pain that frightens you but the knowledge: we're ill-equipped to bear it in these innocent times, and cry out not in agony, but in astonishment at the ordinary, everyday outrage of creation, the beast within that will tear you apart to breathe. Speaking for myself,

I take everything they offer me, the pethidine, the mask over the face, the lot; I'd even have the needle in the back if they suggested it, but apparently, in my case, it's not warranted. Not that their panaceas work: they're completely useless. Pin-pricks in the face of nature's violence. But they do unhinge the mind, which rises giddily, giving vent to a few irreverent home truths, and loses track of itself somewhere up on the neon-lit ceiling.

With Mary I tried to follow their instructions. But now, with my mind out of the way, my body knows better. When they tell me to push I tell them to push off, you can say what you like at such moments. Some stone-age midwife wants me to lie on my side, wants to deliver my baby behind my back: it is, after all, *her* profession. But with Frank as my ambassador I dig in my heels and stay wide-legged and open-eyed on my back. And had I not been in a position to lean forward and grab her, as she slithered head first into view, I might never have believed the child was mine.

She looks at me, still drugged with my pethidine. My blood and my mucus piteously streak her face. But beyond that, she's completely without precedent. She doesn't look like Mary, or her grandmother. This is not a face Frank and I dreamed up; this one comes straight from the angels.

I lie among the mothers in the newly populated night, trying to breathe with propriety. Frank has gone home, but I'm not missing him at all, or remembering the expression in his eyes, exposed as though the hospital mask had slipped, recording without benefit of pencil and paper – or, God be thanked, a camera – images

39

beyond his powers of reproduction. Nor am I thinking of Mary, who's not allowed to come until tomorrow. I'm not identifying with her sense of personal triumph that it's a girl, or anticipating her gratification when she sees her. My focus is all here, in my empty insides, my full breasts, in the ache that I must now account desire. For my darling is in this building, and I am wholly taken up with the wild, the adulterous, passion for the new.

## 11

My mother buys a new hat. She sits in front of a mirror
with a salesgirl ranged behind her, pulling a bendy bit
of felt this way and that. My mother looks wonderful
whichever way it's worn. Her figure has gone, but her
face is untouched by child-bearing. It's hard for me to
see her properly, even though I'm looking at her, even
though she's pulling what she thinks is her definitive
face, the one you always do, in front of the mirror.
Actually her expression hardens at the sight of herself,
so I have to wait for her glance to shift to my face before
I can properly begin to describe hers.

It's not that she's so beautiful. It's just that for me her
face is the original, the one on which my idea of faces is
based. There's something about the disposition of her
features, the space between eye and eyebrow, the
length of the upper lip that makes all other faces, the
salesgirl's, mine, look faintly silly. Despite the admitted
frivolity of the exploit – it's a hat, after all, we're considering – there's a deep and unnerving sobriety in her
eyes.

Where were you planning to wear it? asks the salesgirl, and my mother is stumped. She wasn't planning to

wear the hat at all. She has hundreds of hats, a hat for every occasion; hats for celebration, hats for mourning: every time my father leaves or comes back she buys one and stuffs it in a cupboard with all the others. When you open the doors of her wardrobe they flutter out like birds: hats with brims, hats with veils; feathers, flowers, moths, dust; they all come drifting down over your ducking, bare head and pile up round your ankles like little corpses.

I don't like the bow, I say, and the salesgirl rips it off. She ruins the hat to make my mother happy. As who would not. But my mother has seen another one, over there. Do you think that blue would suit me, Ro? she says. I think any hat in the shop would suit her, but I have to be careful. It's important she goes on liking it all the way home. I do a tour of the millinery department, from head to plaster head; I'm young enough to imagine there might be decapitated bodies in the basement to go with them. When I get back, my mother's got the blue hat on. There's no question in her mind, or the sales-girl's, that this is The One, and I must admit it's an astonishing match with her eyes.

I'll have it, she says, and this is the moment we both love. The salesgirl takes the hat and wraps it tenderly in tissue paper. Then she packs it in a box, which she ties neatly with ribbon, and takes my mother's money with dazzling confidence. The fantasy is that this is a hat with a future. And all the way home on the ferry the feeling stays with us. I carry the hat for my mother: the box warms my lap. She studies the bill with a frown, as though she cares what it cost. I imagine her trying it on again when we get home and showing my father, I imagine his urge to take her out in it, his shock at the price. But he's not there when we get back, and the hat is a disappointment. In the light of the bedroom her eyes are unequal to its blue.

## 12

Just before he left me, I found Frank crying in my cupboard. More of a room, really; you could move around
in there up to a point, between the rails of crammed-
together clothes. Tripped up by trailing skirts and
choked by a chiffon scarf, he was wiping his wet face on
my linen shirtsleeve.

After he'd gone, and taken his own things with him, I
went in there myself to see what it must feel like to be
leaving me. I was so changed, so disfigured by sadness,
that my clothes must have been more redolent of the
woman he once loved than I was. He must have been
upsetting himself at the memory of the way I used to
look, before, as it were, the accident.

There were things in there that I'd had ever since we
met. The cream angora sweater he first put his hand
up. The tight velvet trousers with the zip that he broke
pulling them down. The discreet knitted suit I came off
the plane to meet him in. The louche maternity smock I
wore to our wedding. Brief skirts, and boots that came
half way up the thigh to meet them. No hats, I'm proud
to say, not even for christenings. And there, just like

one of the others, the dress I was wearing when he told me.

Chilling, really, how when all else is faded we women persist in remembering we were all in blue. Or, in this case, brown. I miss her, he said (I forget what he had on at the time). Although it was the middle of the day, he poured me a large neat whisky. He didn't have one himself. It was my grief he wanted to obliterate. He told me he still loved me, and I believed him. But in that careless association he let me make, between alcohol and pain, I saw I was no longer safe with him. He missed her, and the rest was already written. Sooner or later, I would be missing *him*.

Actually, a lot of the clothes in that cupboard were things I'd bought since that day. One of the bonuses of being abandoned is the weight you lose: for the first time in my life I looked better in clothes than out, and I got a bit extravagant, I'm afraid. I matched his passion for her with a passion for spending, as though a cashmere coat might seduce him where I no longer could. He would never have bought such a ritzy thing for her. Not that she would have wanted him to. Apparently she prided herself on looking good on a shoe-string (or was it in a G-string?). And was happiest, so he said, in a T-shirt and jeans.

Maybe I mistook Frank's reason for raking through the past. Maybe what he was mourning was not its charm, but its arrant wastefulness. I had some whimsical idea he had a foetal desire to stay shut inside my cupboard for ever. But probably all he was doing in the claustrophobic gloom was working up the anger to go.

## 13

My father doesn't always leave home *from* home, so to speak. Sometimes he disappears right in the middle of an outing. You look round, there's nobody there: that's my father. And there's a meal to finish, or the rest of a musical to get through. My mother sits straight-backed, loyal consort to an empty seat. Daddy'shadtogobackto-theoffice is passed down the row. But your appetite has gone, or the plot abruptly ceases to make sense. The waiters change their manner (can my mother pay the bill?), their servility dependent on male grandeur. Or up on the screen a saintly woman sings of her helpless, hopeless bondage to some bastard.

*What's the use of wund'ring* (you think to yourself), *If he's good or if he's bad, Or if you like the way he wears his hat?* And you do like it, you do; that's the awful thing: the way he wears his hat is half the trouble. Because if these musicals are anything to go by, the bastard is always the hero, with his propensity to cheat and strut about. Baritone though he be, if not the bald King of Siam, he's just a little boy at heart.

*He may not always do, What you would have him do; Then all at once he'll do, Something, wonderful.* And that is what we are waiting for, my mother and I. For my father to do something wonderful. And his ability to do that depends for some reason, on our faith.

*He has a thousand dreams, that won't come true, You know that he believes in them, and that's enough for you.* And it is. It really is. Because if he doesn't believe, the inference is he will die. And what he will die of is our scepticism. Our terrible female failure to comprehend that he really means well. I'm twelve, but I know this to be true. So that when he disappears into the night without a word, I am fearful for no less than his life.

## 14

Catastrophe, which once would have dawned on us in stages, through a clever build-up of atmosphere – the premonitory barking of dogs, the distant drumbeat of hooves, the white face of a messenger – comes to us now out of a clear blue sky by the brisk means of the telephone.

Don't answer it, says Frank, but he's already hauling himself to his feet.

It'll be for you, I say, but I follow him into the house. It was our way, in those days, to do everything together. After the glare of the garden we're suddenly plunged into gloom, but I'm not warned. I stand there smiling, all ears, since I can hardly see; I usually guess who's on the line from the way Frank says hello. The desk is piled with books and papers, he has to fumble for the phone: she starts screaming before he can get the receiver to his ear.

Don't do that, he says, to whatever it is she's shrieking. I really wouldn't do that, if I were you.

When he hangs up, he tries to pretend it was his agent. That was my agent, he says, although his agent's name is Patrick, and since when did he earn his percentage in a screaming falsetto? Also, Frank has failed to replace the receiver properly, despite his eyes being accustomed now to the light. I do it for him, but he knocks it off again. Leave it alone, he says savagely, Don't you dare touch it. Meaning Mary, Edith, this house, our marriage, everything.

But I can't leave it alone. I have to go on and on until he tells me.

You *know*, he says accusingly when he's run out of bluster (What? Are you mad? How dare you! When? Who?). And he's right: I've known about the mad bitch all along. The dogs *did* bark, the hooves *did* drum, the pallor of the messenger was unmistakable. (Who's this? said Mary, shoving Frank's very first drawing of her under my nose.) You might even say the whole thing was my idea. Is she pretty, I'd said, this woman who's going to interview you for television? And then, when I saw the transmission: Don't try to tell me she didn't make a pass at you! They do, don't they, nowadays, women like that? (Women like what? Like I once was? Fuck you as soon as look at you?) You might even say I put the whole idea into his head. Picked the person, wrote the script myself, suspected him with so much dogged conviction that it must have seemed to him unsporting in the end, not to let my hypothesis have its way. And yet now that he's proved me right, I'm completely wrong-footed. You see, all the time I knew, I had no idea.

Frank, who always puts things oddly, in his own, one-off way, suddenly starts picking his words as if from some common fund of portentous expressions. There *is* Someone Else, he says, and for a moment my heart lifts: perhaps he means there's someone other than her. Someone whose face I don't recognize in my blood, who hasn't already come into my dreams, who isn't already invested with the power of my hatred. But he says her name, Linda. Actually, it's not her name, but I don't know that yet, any more than she knows that my name isn't Rosa. Her name, if you please, is the same as mine, Rosalind. On opposite sides of the world our mothers got the same bright idea at the sight of us. But we don't know that yet, any of us, least of all Frank. He's serenely unaware of being referee in a vulgar scuffle for identity. For the moment it's bad enough that her name is as stupid as Linda; if I allow such a word near my tongue, my saliva may turn to acid and rot my teeth.

So I just stand there, duped, my mother to the life. And he stares back, unmasked, my own true enemy. And my great grief is that I know we will never recover from this moment. A crime has been committed here that cannot be forgiven, and that crime is the original one of innocence. I am guilty of too much faith. Despite the old-eyed sense of corruption I was born with, I have conducted myself in my married life like a child. Now he'll never forgive me. Men never forgive the women they betray. Oh, *I'll* get over it, I'll condone everything, love him more, if anything, with mellower, more womanly eyes, because what is he but a man and what are men but faithless, faithless to the last, and how we thrive on that, we condescending bitches, how we crave to have something to forgive. But he won't forgive me. I'll always be the woman he did this to; this ordinary, mundane, inevitable, insupportable thing. And in the end he'll want to be rid of me. Rid of the memory of the look on my face when I found out. I shouldn't have made him suffer it, that last dumb, trusting, sleepy smile of mine before the sudden rupture of the dream. It happens to everyone. I of all people should have known that: it happened to my mother, it happened to his first wife, it is life, for heaven's sake, nothing personal. Except that it *is* personal now that it's happened to me. That is the trick of it: it happens every time for the first time; the blood and the astonishment are undimmed.

Frank has a terrible look on his face at the sight of what has become of me already. I'm insanely unhappy, but it's worse than that. I have come, in some sinister way, into my inheritance. This is the world as I always knew it to be, vigorous with betrayal, and that tranquillity I once had, five minutes ago, was a trance he rocked me into, a dummy he kept in my mouth for ten long years to stop me howling. But I'm wide awake now, and full of primal energy; what is over for him is just beginning for me. Tell me, I say, and it's all I ever do say from now on: What was she like, what is it like with her, tell me.

At first he's seduced by being able actually to say it. We were so used to telling each other everything, it was as though things only happened to us for the purpose of being passed on; the dullest detail of his day was always flailing around, trying to whip itself into an anecdote for me, to make me giggle and gasp and say how riveting. And then it happened, the thing he couldn't mention. He's been coming back from London for months now, dying to flop down in his favourite chair with the latest, Hey, guess what happened today, I fucked this girl.

Well, I'm riveted all right, and gasping, the perfect

audience. Except that I'm having a bit of trouble seeing the funny side. I mean it's serious, the woman obviously loves him. You can always tell a really loving woman by the damage she's prepared to wreak around her. What else but love would prompt her to come screaming down the phone, threatening to tell me, or kill herself? Well, I know about her now, so the first option's gone – hadn't he better forestall her from trying the second?

But it's clear, from the way he's not leaping into the car and tearing down the motorway to her side, that where states of mind are concerned, mine is the one he considers the more precarious; although we both know *I* won't kill myself: *that* road is closed to me for ever, that is a thing I would die rather than do. And the tragedy is that I'm still too childishly ignorant, too wife-ishly arrogant, to see that this is triumph, this is happiness: he actually rates my neurosis over hers.

He's following me about, trying to feel his way to what he can say to make it better for me. The necessity to make it better for him doesn't occur to me. I'm too taken up with roaming from room to room, making new associations wherever I go, infecting the whole house with my fever, trying out the novelty of my pain leaning against this piece of furniture, looking at that picture, seeing from which once-loved object, what polished or stained or swathed surface, the surge of suffering is strongest. Luckily Edith's having her afternoon nap and Mary's being picked up from school by another, saner mother, and there are only the dogs to bump into, because I'm frightened of anything animate, terrified of being taken by surprise, of having my concentration broken, since the piercing line of what I'm attending to is taking up all my effort; if a child were to approach me at random, with a random demand for something childish, I might harden my heart against her, I might scream at her to leave me alone.

Tell me what to do, says Frank, and I'm thinking hard, trying to work out what it is I want from him (he is the person, after all, I always turn to), and what I seem to need most is information, illumination, after having being kept for so long in the dark. In fact that now seems to be my grudge: not what he's done but that he's left me behind, and gone ahead and done it without me.

It's not just dates and times I want, but visual and textural disclosures, I want sights, smells, sound effects, the look on her face when she comes: that is the price I'm already exacting, that he deliver her up to me in detail, in the sticky, slippery, fallible, goose-pimpled flesh. I'm still obsessed with colour schemes, although I've seen enough on television of the kind of heightened pigmentation effects she sports to imagine to what tawny tones her naked nipples aspire. And although I was on the right track about her hair, which turns out to be a carroty shade of corn, can he clear up the question of the fleece? Is it the gold Jason dreamed of, or just a dank, especially when damp, unretouched, unremarkable shade of mouse?

But he won't tell me, or rather tries to, but can't; hasn't noticed or something, was cross-eyed at the time, lovers being I suppose so close to each other when they're together that everything is just a blur of bodies, a juxtaposition of juices. And this sudden silence of his, this discovery of a loyalty he didn't know he had, frightens us both, is our first intimation that the day will soon come when we would settle for wishing ourselves no further back into the past than this, to the time just after I found out, before the real damage began to be done. But Edith has woken up and is crying her anguished cry at the abandonment she is convinced all babies are heir to, and Mary is at the door, wants her tea, has seen my face, and time has moved inexorably on.

## 15

My mother prepares a picnic. She shaves off the pitted, picked-at sides of some old fruit cake she's found and forms it into respectable oblong pieces which she wraps in greaseproof paper. Packed lunches are not usually her strong point. When people at school swap sandwiches I pretend I'm too mean to share mine, I show not the faintest flicker of interest in their peanut butter and jam, or curried egg and watercress, or salami and gherkin, even when they flip up the corner of one of their expertly cut triangles with the crusts indulgently trimmed off, to see what they're being tempted with today, confident it will be something desirable, so confident they can afford to be disgusted: Eugh! Look what Mum's given me this time, cream cheese and pineapple!

I know what's going to be in my sandwiches before I unwrap them, before I've even taken them out of their brown-paper bag: the remains of the roast meat from the weekend, garnished with slices of leaky tomato. Or towards the end of the week, just the tomato. Actually, she did surprise me once: she left out the bread. Perhaps we had run out, or she was sick of sawing away at the left-over lamb, but in the strange shaped paper parcel I found nothing but bones. I had to hide behind the lavatories to gnaw them. It never occurred to me to throw them away – it's part of the faith I keep with my mother that I always eat everything she gives me, even the crusts which of course she leaves on (when she remembers the bread, that is). I munch to the very last crumb, however much the butter is tainted with the taste of undefrosted fridge, however soggy the bread has turned from the tomato seeping pinkly through its pores (encouraged by the weight with which she leans on the layers to cut her uncompromising squares). My sandwiches have been squashed by my books, I say, fostering my reputation for insularity, eating under cover of my brown paper bag, destroying the evidence by mouth.

So I'm standing here, amazed by my mother, at the care she's suddenly taking with this fruit cake, trimming off the collapsing bits, wrapping it as though it were a present. It's not as if we're going to the beach. We can't go anywhere this weekend: my father's going off in the car with some colleague – the picnic, she explains, is for him. Or rather, Them. She's found a proper basket in the cellar with an old flask in it and bits of looped elastic in the lid to hold the knives and forks. I take advantage of her excitement to try to teach her how to be a proper housewife, and for once she complies: she actually dusts the spiders out of the basket and looks on approvingly as I rinse out the mouldy old flask until the water runs reasonably transparent.

What'll we give them to drink? she says, and I suggest lemon squash, although it's obvious my father will want whisky at the very least: this is *our* treat, my mother's and mine. I've got ideas for what to put in the sandwiches too – all those pent-up dreams of what a mother might think of. Tuna fish, I cry. On brown bread, with mayonnaise! And in seconds I've got my sandals on and am rushing down to the local shop for ingredients. When I get back there's some frustration over the whereabouts of a tin opener, but my mother is inspired and locates one, although she cuts herself slightly in her excitement, struggling with its back and forth action.

Let me do it, I say, you'll get blood on the bread, and she giggles and lets me, sucking her finger, marvelling at my strange, responsible ways. What about some tomato? she says, but I shake my head firmly: no red, oozy juices of any sort.

Some cucumber would be nice, I say, and miraculously she produces one, not too shrivelled and bitter, from the depths of the fridge. She allows me to wash it and throw the soggy end away, and its dark-rimmed slices look nice against the delicate mashed-up flesh colour of the fish. On the top slice of bread I press with the utmost lightness, but when it comes to the cutting I'm nervous. I don't want to hurt her, I don't want to undermine her with the knowledge that there are such exotic things abroad in the world as triangles. But my knife turns diagonally as if on a whim of its own: these sandwiches must at all events be pretty. And in fact she's delighted. That's perfect! she cries. And the crusts off too, what daintiness! And there's a note in her voice which somehow manages to undermine me, as though there's something about triangles that's in poorer taste than I thought; as though there's a joke in the presentation of this food that I'm not getting. Next she wants me to pick flowers – pink ones, please, camellias – and though I'm eager enough to do her bidding, I'm no longer as happy as I should be; I'm not humming as I dodge the bees in the bushes, although I'm allowed to pick the blooms with the buds.

When Daddy's friend arrives, says my mother, you give the flowers to her, darling. Say: Mummy and I made this picnic specially for you; say: I hope you and Daddy really enjoy it.

And then above the flowers I sense my father standing there in his freshly ironed white shirt. And I can tell from his crushed, white face that he's not hungry.

## 16

On our first outing, the man who wants to be my first
lover takes me on a picnic. He doesn't bring a basket
with him; he says we can get something there. By there
he means the beach, as people always do in Sydney,
and although I've just sailed the breadth of the harbour
to meet him, he takes me on the ferry, the big one, the
Manly one, which goes out past the Heads within reach
of the open sea. I'm fifteen and he thinks it's a treat he's
giving me, it doesn't occur to him that to me these boats
are just public transport, about as exotic as a tram or a
bus or a train. It's a treat for him though, he can't get
over it, the thrill of getting about the place by water.
He's from England, a Ten Pound Pom, he can't get over
the incessant sunshine either, although the day he
chooses for this picnic turns out to be dull and grey.
What he doesn't realize is that dullness *is* a treat for me:
I'm perverse about my country, I like it on its off days; I
hate the hard reflected brightness that makes me screw
up my eyes.

As I've mentioned before, my Englishman's name is
Alfred. I can't imagine why he feels he has to stick to
such a name. Surely the point of changing countries is

that you can call yourself what you like. I wonder what he's left behind, what lives, what wives, what havoc. This is the land of opportunity, but coming out here as a migrant still seems to denote some sort of failure, an ambition not realized, a connection best forgotten. He fields personal questions with jokes and funny voices; he can do any accent, Welsh, Liverpudlian, two kinds of Scottish; the only one he can't seem to manage is my own – his attempts at the local lingo come out like curdled Cockney. He seems to think it will amuse me to have the foibles of my countrymen sent up to my face, and he's right, it does; the feminine response he calls up in me (a boyish, boisterous belly laugh) knows no loyalty, even to itself. In the welter of assumed voices I can't pin down his real one, I know nothing of his background, and to be honest I don't care to; it's enough for me that he's foreign, it's enough for me that he's thirty, it's enough that my father would have a fit if he knew I was out for the day with him.

Not that there's anything to worry about. We're not alone. I've brought my friend Nancy along for company and protection. But we're hardly out of the harbour before I'm seriously regretting it. Nancy has taken her role of chaperone to heart. She's there at my elbow, laughing louder than anyone at Alfred's jokes. She's shorter and more thickset than I am, but that hasn't stopped her coming as my twin. She's wearing exactly the same as I am, the same pedal-pushers and tucked-in sweater, the same pulled-back hair-do with wisps coming loose round the forehead, the same ingratiating grin. Alfred doesn't take the likeness into account. His jokes are for my laughter only; he uses her as background, something to pick me out from. And I find that I'm not kind to her in his company, although it's I who've begged her to come on this trip in the first place. I connive with him against her, catch his eye over the top of her head, send her away with sixpence to get us a packet of peanuts. But as soon as she's out of sight, shyness strikes me, I haven't the faintest idea what to say to him; you'd think the sun had come out and was blinding me from the way I start squinting and shading my eyes with my hand. It's the same shyness I sometimes feel with my father, but what feels so different about Alfred, what is making me so deliriously happy, is to be with a man who doesn't love me. Alfred isn't interested in my spirit. He isn't trying to *claim* me in some way. Despite the awkward silence between us, it's beginning to fill me with a sense of profound security that all this stranger really wants to do is fuck me. His shirtsleeves are rolled back to the elbow and the thick blond hairs on his forearms stand out with a kind of static excitement from his skin; I'm moved by the callow, angular line from his jaw to his ear. The urge to touch him is so natural it's almost motherly, but at my early stage of life you have to keep such feelings strictly to yourself. Single drops of water keep flicking into my face; I'm not sure whether they're coming from the sky or the sea. Not that it makes any difference to my sense of refreshment: gazing out over the horizon with a man who barely knows me at my side, I feel on the verge of some important maritime discovery. And then he goes and spoils it all by speaking.

Your friend's laugh is really annoying, he says. I wish you could have come on this trip by yourself. And sud-

61

denly all my loyalties are to Nancy, whose laugh, an endearing copy of my own, will have me helpless on the floor before he ever will. I start looking around for her wildly, as though I'll faint any minute for lack of a peanut, and sure enough, here she comes, negotiating the rolling deck with her bouncy walk. And no sooner do I set eyes on her than I'm wishing her overboard all over again: God, I say when it turns out she's got crisps, it was all they had, honestly, Nancy, *really*. She starts to scoff them herself, but has trouble swallowing. It's beginning to become clear even to her that her presence on this trip is counter-productive. I grow bold with Alfred just because she's watching; by the time we get off at Manly he and I are holding hands.

We let each other go to eat ice-creams in the street: I think I can taste his palm on my cone. Nancy, licking hers sedately from the top, takes a dim view of the way I bite a hole in the bottom of mine and suck the soft stuff through. I kick my sandals off when we get to the sand, knowing that Alfred will carry them. She keeps hers on, knowing that he won't carry hers; I'm aware of the sinking splendour of my feet. It's so grey a day there's hardly anyone on the beach, but Alfred is scornful of the surf, I think he's afraid the waves will show up his Englishness. He wants to *swim* he says (I'll bet he's a whizz at breaststroke). He's prepared to walk for miles round the coastline to a tiny sheltered cove called Fairy Bay: he doesn't seem to mind the connotation. Nor do I. I like anything he likes, even sharks, which Nancy predicts will get us if we stray so far from the lifeguards.

By the time we reach Alfred's chosen bit of beach it's way past lunch-time, and we're miles from any food, but who cares, we're boiling, all we want to do is fall into the water. We've got our bathers on under our clothes and we strip down unceremoniously, where we stand. Nancy's bikini is red with white dots. She's bigger busted than I am, with a more nipped-in waist, but I can tell Alfred prefers my flatter chest, my longer thighs, my plain black one-piece. As for him, I'm amazed at his undressed beauty. The arch of his rib-cage makes me want to cry. To go with his old-fashioned bathing trunks he has a wonderful foreign pallor, which he rushes to hide in the sea, striking out towards the horizon with a surprisingly accomplished crawl. Nancy and I plunge in after him, but as soon as it's deep enough I swim off in a sideways direction; what with there being no way out of my underclothes on the long ferry trip, I'm bursting for a pee. I've hardly finished going when suddenly Alfred surfaces beside me, immersed in my water, the undispersed warmth of it. Does he know? Can he tell? I'm up to my neck, but my face must give it away: the water turns hotter from my blushing: the only way out of this soup I'm in must be to drown in it. But he gets there first – with eyes wide open in an expression of unimagined frankness, he dis-appears under the cloudy water where I'm standing. And in that extraordinary moment of baptism, sud-denly everything depends on the fact that he *does* know, knows but doesn't care, *wants* to plunge his face into my murky secretions; I feel his head butting between my thighs where the heat is still most concentrated, the ammonia still most stinging, and all at once he's lifting me, I'm sitting on his shoulders like an astonished bal-lerina as he bursts back through the surface, spouting polluted streams from his nose and ears and mouth. And he runs with me like that, in slow motion, the way you're forced to against the weight of water, towards the shore, while spotted Nancy bobs up and down in the shallows, making waves of disapproval all of her own. And when he collapses with me on to the foamy sea floor my muscles ache with the sudden release of tension, as though it's not he who has been bearing me on his back, but I who have borne his head between my thighs.

So that later, when he puts his hand there, when we've swum ourselves to a standstill and are lying flaked out on the sand, I'm primed, I don't take it amiss, as I might if he made the slightest attempt to kiss me; his touch feels tame and unassuming after the straining, bullish ferocity of his neck. Besides, his hand just seems to wander there in the vague, disembodied way I like so much, as though he instinctively knows this truth about me, that my cunt is more accessible than I am. True, he's murmuring poetry at the time (T. S. Eliot, of all unlikely aphrodisiacs – one up on his later choice of Doris Day), but more I think to bore me than engage me, as though to awaken my instincts by dulling my brain. My mother is a writer and my father a philanderer, but it's obvious he considers me a complete ignoramus in matters of poetry and sex. And he's right, I am, but his assumption isn't patronizing, it's reverential. He holds my uninitiated body and vacant mind in holy esteem. Nothing is required of me, no knowledge, no expertise; all I have to do is be what I am, a girl. I lie *like a patient etherized upon a table*; I suppose I should be ashamed, but I'm not, there's a curious glory in the complete abnegation of my will, and besides, Alfred's hand inside my swimsuit poses no threat to me; the threat (and there is one) comes not from what men might do to me, but from what women would say if they knew: Nancy, for instance, that tireless mermaid out there, still bobbing up and down unsinkably in the sea. My most fervent response to his caresses is the wish that she should stay there, not so much out of the sight of his disappearing hand, as out of earshot of his J. Alfred Prufrock.

*Do I dare to eat a peach*? The question seems rhetorical from where I'm lying, with my bottom clenched against the hardening sand. He recites without inflection, in imitation, if I but knew it, of the author's own drawling monotone; the question marks are all in his hooking, pin-pointing forefinger. I don't say yes or no by so much as a whimper, it doesn't seem to be my place to answer: the flesh and juice of my body are as abstract to me as they are to him. As fast as I'm drying off from the outside in I'm getting damp from the inside out. I want him to kiss me now, my mouth is lax and avid for what seems like the culmination of these preliminaries, but as he rolls towards me, here comes Nancy, sprinting up the sand to take charge of my honour. We roll apart, hating her; it's the strongest mutual emotion we've felt so far and it binds us together dangerously: from now on we're bent on delinquency.

We ought to go, she says in the nagging tone we have somehow thrust upon her. Look, the tide's coming in: if we don't go now we'll be stranded.

She's right – nags always are – it's quite exciting: we have to scale a few rocks to get past the rising water. I'm a born rock climber, I've shinned up some really craggy ones in my time with my athletic father, leaving my sisters sitting on the sand, too fat or frightened to follow. The sense of being his tomboy, his darling, is with me now as I scramble ahead of Nancy, scorning Alfred's help. Wait for me, she keeps calling, but Alfred and I take no notice; we're too busy exploring the rocks ahead for the hidden places, the jutting out bits with gullies in between, smooth and slimy, dark scented, salt tasting, and still he's only kissed my mouth in passing.

By the time we're out on to open beach again there's the best part of a hundred yards between us: looking back I have a suspicion that Nancy is crying.

Wait for her, I tell Alfred. Include her. Be nice to her. And we turn and wait as she comes self-consciously towards us, the bounce in her step more of a limp in the soggy sand. Alfred's idea of being nice to people is to put his arm round them, flirt a little, and I must say it works like a charm: before long she's carrying his sandals as well as mine and her own. He grows friendlier and friendlier, it amuses him to prove that her disapproval was just jealousy all along. I'm getting a bit disapproving myself: once we reach the street I stalk on ahead, we can't stay a threesome for more than a few minutes. It's beginning to get dark and I start lingering outside restaurants, claiming to be hungry, although I'm not, not for food, I can't sustain two appetites at once. We end up in a scruffy dive with dirty tables and neon lights, eating fish and chips and drinking beer. I hate beer. Normally I have to hold my breath just at the smell of it, but tonight I'm an initiate, I'm open to anything: the thought of it foaming down Alfred's gullet, lingering on his breath, makes me want to swill it round in my own mouth, dare to swallow. And it's not bad in sips; in fact after a few goes I'm quite greedy for it. Although it's the national drink and deeply identified in my psyche with the blue-nosed belching drunks who leer across the landscape of my childhood, tonight it tastes foreign, exotic even, by sweet association with Alfred's digestive tract, as though a lifetime's prejudice, whole cultures, could be wiped from one's experience by the sudden omnipotent onset of desire. The fact is that Alfred is more at home in this café than we are: we might as well be in his country, as he in ours. As for me, I've never before clapped eyes on a menu with no greens on it, or had vinegar on my fish instead of lemon, or fed money into a jukebox that blares out Johnnie Ray, or in short been anywhere so thrillingly proletarian in my life. I suddenly have a vision of an existence where no standard is too low, no food or shelter is to be scorned: it's the closest I come with Alfred to falling in love. But luckily I'm still enough of a child to know what's what; love is a fuzz round the face so you can't see the person for the surfeit of your feeling, and I can see what Alfred is quite clearly: a man with a weird propensity for the company of schoolgirls.

And Nancy and I give him what he wants. We regale him with stories of our teachers: Miss West, who, the lavatory wall tells us, is a pest (Wet her pants in an English test), and Miss O'Connor, who has ill-fitting teeth and advises us when we stand as she enters to Shit, girlsh.

For the length of the meal our triangle is a success, with Alfred laughing in a strangely high-pitched tone in an attempt to pass himself off as our contemporary. But on the ferry going home he and Nancy grow moody again; she boringly so, he rather frighteningly, his hairline descending even lower with his wrath. We sit in a row looking out to sea; there's no one out on the deck in the dark but us. The unspoken quarrel is back to what it was in the first place, a tug-of-war over me and what is left of my virtue. Nancy doesn't stand a chance. Smelling stirringly of fried fish in the salt night air, Alfred presses his thick thigh hard against mine. The more he edges towards me, the more she, sitting on my other side, must move along. Finally he manoeuvres her right off the end of the bench: she's forced to get up and go and sit on the other side of him, and then he turns his back on her altogether. Why do I let him? Why don't I get up, change places, push him off, ally myself with her as she does with me? I don't know. I don't care. I want her to go away so that he can kiss me. I am filled with the power of knowing how much he wants to, and fascinated to see how he'll solve the problem. Actually his solution is simple but inspired; he kisses me in order to make her go away. He turns my face towards him with the flat of one hand, that being all it takes, and cocking his head in a calculated, excitingly unimpassioned way, coolly draws my whole mouth into his. He doesn't pretend to tenderness just because she's watching, but bites and sucks quite fiercely at my lips which have never opened to anyone before. Over his shoulder, through my closing eyelids, I see Nancy, looking seasick, get up and wander aimlessly away. And part of me goes after her, puts an arm round her, laughs it off, hates men, is a child again, while the rest of me is his for ever, just to feel the hot insistence of his tongue.

He keeps the kiss up for an inordinate length of time, teaching me the fluttering gamut of his tricks, while the ferry imitates my insides as it lurches and pitches through the rough stretch of sea between the Heads. And when Nancy comes back, there's nothing I don't know about the way he wants to make love to me that his mouth hasn't already graphically suggested; nothing that will pass between us that hasn't been pre-empted by the trail of his thick saliva still wet on my chin.

Nancy sits down two benches away from us: I can tell from the hunch of her shoulders that she's thrown up. But I am well, and will be well despite her; the effect of love seems to be to harden the heart. I'm already planning the lies I'll have to tell her: my mother's ill, I've developed this sudden interest in maths. I'll tell her anything, even the truth if necessary – that friendship is dead and I don't give a damn what becomes of me, only next time a man asks me out, I'm going alone.

## 17

Today is my day for leaving, says Frank, as though abandoning his wife and children were a long-standing commitment that might have slipped his mind if he hadn't made a responsible note of it in his diary. His tone is so light and unemphatic that I might not have grasped his meaning at all, were he not staggering out of the bedroom at the time with his whole life apparently stuffed into two suitcases. He has never packed before without my help and advice, and this independent sorting out of socks and shirts and underpants strikes me as a terrible betrayal. Normally a fairly gentle, soft-voiced woman, I begin to scream in a lusty, unremitting tone, which shocks him badly.

Don't make that noise, says Frank, or I won't be able to go. He needs me to smooth the path for him as I always have in the past. And perhaps, as I continue to scream, that is what I'm doing. For it's true that no sane person could stay in the vicinity of such a racket. It's not an adult sound I'm making, it's like the mad bawling of a baby: his male instinct retreats from it in clumsiness and fear. His real baby, Edith, joins in from an adjoining room, and he puts down his suitcases, all too ready to go to her to try to hush her. But I get there first, and pick her up and cling to her for what feels like my own protection, and our two faces face him, female, immemorial, as if he were forsaking all women, everywhere.

But in making us cry, he's making some other woman ecstatically happy. Go to her, then, I scream (he's going anyway); and then – Don't go (as if anything's going to stop him now). I get round in front of him; I want to throw something down, break something precious at his feet, but I can't, I've got the baby in my arms. I imagine Edith's skull cracking open on the floor; he ought not to leave a madwoman in charge of his children. But today is his day for leaving, so he pushes on past me, heaving his bags down the stairs, out of the door, into the boot. He drives off, slowly at first because of the pot-holes, with me stumbling along in his wake, trying to catch him up, holding out the baby as black-mail, like beggars do, begging him to stay, calling out his name, a left woman for all the countryside to see. For fifty, maybe a hundred yards I maintain my position, bobbing up and down in his rear-view mirror. But even as I run, I know the image is wrong; it's not coming out the way I'm feeling it. The figure I'm cutting isn't pitiful at all: watchers at the windows of the cottages in the lane are witnessing something altogether different. Even with the weight of the child hanging round my neck, my speed and my stamina are quite awesome. As though what we have here is not a man leaving his wife, but a woman driving her husband away.

## 18

Daddy's gone, says my mother, standing over me, fully dressed, hat and all, at three o'clock in the morning. I don't know whether she's in my dream or out of it. But the more I wake up, the more the nightmare grows. You'll have to come with me, she says, I'm afraid something's happened to your father. We may need someone small to climb through the office window.

I don't question that the someone must be me. I *am* small; well, not short, I suppose, but skinny, and completely unencumbered by those obstacles to adventure: breasts. How would my elder sister force hers through a tight office window? And my younger sister needs looking after; I can see that. I'm a miles better climber than I am a baby-sitter. But I have this sudden fear of falling. I feel sick. I can't even do up my buttons. I wanted to be left asleep; now that I'm awake, I want at least to be left in the light. It's dark outside, I want to stay in the house, but I can't, I have to go and help look for my father. And my chest constricts with the fear of what we may find.

An employee of my father's is waiting for us in the street. His name is Caj, he's Dutch, he drives a van. His face is pink: a foreigner's embarrassing sunburn, or high blood pressure at the mortal struggle he's having with English. He's keen to be up at this ungodly hour justifying his job, which is delivering things to the office: tonight we're his load. He's old for a messenger boy, so he wants us to know he's doing this partly out of friendship; as we rattle three abreast through the empty streets, he jabbers on about how wonderful my father was and how he looked up to him, and I don't know if he's got his tenses wrong, or if he is a true messenger of doom. My mother doesn't answer or even listen; her face is turned away, she's gazing out of the window. She and I are in a particular kind of pain which suspends any sense we once had of time and distance. The journey, unhindered by traffic on the bridge or queues at the toll gate, must be taking ten minutes at most, when at peak hour it might take fifty, but each moment, each mile, is absurdly drawn out, exists outside the jurisdiction of maps or clocks. There are red lights at which we must come to a full stop as though in obedience to some unyielding law of punctuation, since no one in the depths of this dead city has the least desire to cross in front of our path. I'm sitting in the middle anyway, but I don't share my mother's dedication to the scenery. The night has a dangerous air of being out and about, up to things, when nobody human is looking; I don't raise my eyes to it much except to save myself from car sickness, or to check the name of the street we're passing through. My father's office is in Hunter Street; Caj, used to having to triple park to make his deliveries, pulls up with unsuitable satisfaction outside the front entrance.

There's a light on the third floor, just as my mother

suspected. He's there. It's sure. My legs don't work too well: I'm no good for shinning up drainpipes. It's all I can do to support myself leaning against my mother. But Caj turns out to be a hero. He's eager to be the one to break into this building. It's not just that he looks up to my father, who at six foot four has that effect on everyone who works for him; it's that he wants to demonstrate the skills he's brought from Holland, the feats he can perform that don't involve the use of language. He's a brilliant burglar, for instance. He's up the fire escape as soon as look at him, across the roof and dropping down through a skylight he's kicked a hole in.

My mother and I cross the road for a better view. We stand under the yellow awning of a pineapple-crush bar, craning upwards as though my father were halfway to heaven already. After a while the cramp in our necks is rewarded; more lights come on on the third floor, and Caj appears, gesticulating, at one of the windows.

Come down, calls my mother, let me in. But he keeps on waving. His frenzied mime seems to evoke a whole cast of cowboys and Indians, although my mother and I both know that the drama that has been enacted here tonight has been a one-man show. Come down, she calls again. There's another long pause. What is the idiot Dutchman doing up there? I'm for following him up the fire escape: climbing seems easy now in the face of waiting. But my mother hangs on to me fiercely; it's hard to tell which of us is shaking, we seem plugged into the same source of current; the air is hot, but we're shivering, my mother and I. Or else it's cold, and we're burning with some shared fever. My mother says, Oh God, again and again. And my prayer is really for an

74

end, any end to what I don't understand. And as if in answer, the night suddenly screams with sirens, and as Caj shoots its heavy bolts and throws it open, an ambulance and two police cars sweep up to the door.

My mother gives a cry and rushes across the road. She's into the building before the police can intercept her. I stay where I am: to be honest, it's all I'm brave enough to do. Caj, brushed aside by the police, and stung by my mother's unexpected anger, looks round for somewhere to put what remains of his heroism: lit up in the yellow shop front, he sees me. He crosses the road and tries to put an arm around my shoulder. Compared to the adults I'm used to, he's not very tall. But I'm angry, like my mother, at whatever it is he's done to offend her: panicked, phoned the authorities, given the game away. Nor do I want his proxy, pink-faced protection; his paternal impulse fills me with dread and desolation, I'll have my own father, thanks all the same, or no one.

Is he dead? I ask coldly; the answer seems to be no. Or not quite. Nearly. Would have been, had we not arrived in time. Caj is so busy trying to make clear what happened he forgets he's talking to a child. And it's easy enough to understand what is not for your ears. My father swallowed pills with a bottle of whisky and was sick. Shot himself drunkenly with a hand-held revolver and missed. Would have fallen on a blunt sword, no doubt, if he hadn't passed out. And now he's being carried indecorously into the street. I can't help it, I bury my face in Caj's coat. By the time I look up they've already got the stretcher in the ambulance. But the police are detaining my mother. She's not just the victim's wife, you see, she's the murderer's accomplice; I rush across the street to her side. But she's in her element, elated: my father is alive. To her he's redeemed, she's brought him back from the dead. There's nothing they can say that can harm her: it's they, in fact, who have fallen into her hands. There's no need for there to be a record of this, is there? she says. I can see, now, her point in stopping to put on a hat. One look at her felt-framed madonna face and they capitulate. Their chief tears up the written report on the spot: he'll personally make sure not a breath of this reaches the press.

My mother takes Caj, who's joined us, by the hand. Thank you, she says. What would we have done without you? I take his other hand after all, because I know she would want me to. We're going to need his services again to drive us to the hospital.

But the next day my mother wears her hat in vain. In or out of it, my father doesn't want to see her. With his stomach pumped and his grazed temple adorned with sticking plaster, he refuses to set eyes on his saviour. A nurse comes up to us with the message that the only person he's prepared to see is me.

It's an honour I could do without. Especially as my mother is now flanked by my two sisters, who look at me as though I were Cinderella: if my father is their prince, they can have him. But my mother's blue eyes are unflinching; she's so strong in this crisis that she refuses to interpret anything as a setback: she's already seeing me as her better chance, a purer vessel for her selfless love than she is. Tell him how much we need him, she instructs me. Make him understand we have to have him back.

I'm guided between the rows of beds by the nurse. On closer inspection she's not a nurse, she's a nun. But my father is not a Roman Catholic. It comes to me that this is not a proper hospital. This is a place of sanctuary for drunkards and deadbeats: no one here apart from my father has shaved for a week. But then of course my father's not a proper patient. He hasn't fallen ill with a respectable, God-given disease. He's committed a crime, an act of self-violation; the police may be prepared to forget it, but these nuns are not. There's nothing in the world more implacable than an angel of mercy: this one has glasses and doesn't particularly like little girls. She's used to ministering to the sort of men nobody would dream of visiting, not ones like my father, with his stream of attendant women.

Because when we get there, there's one already sitting on his bed. I wasn't the only person he was prepared to see, after all. Her name turns out to be some month – May, June. July. I hate her, whatever her season, with a black passion, even though at the back of my mind there's a small, shameful surge of relief that I'm not going to be left alone to cope with a madman. For to my utter and everlasting horror, my father is crying. He cries quietly and unceasingly throughout the interview. My mother's messages go completely out of my head. Don't be so stupid, I whisper. Don't be so stupid. But he looks at me with eyes that might never have seen me again and pulls me towards him: I'm expected to kiss his wet cheek. Even a day's growth of beard can be shocking on a man of his vanity. Vanity –

what am I talking about? – he has none left. He starts to say dreadful, slurred things in a broken voice, hoarse from the pipe they have had to force down his throat. Made such a hash of it, he says. Couldn't even get that right. Why wouldn't she leave me to die? Why did she have to drag me back?

How can I discuss my mother's actions in front of this woman? She looks on smugly as if to prove the superiority of her love by agreeing with every word my father's saying. Shh, I say, Daddy, don't *talk* like that. We *had* to. You can't just let people . . . You have to try and stop them from . . .

Why? he says. Why? What for? And for a moment his logic holds sway. There's such yearning in his voice, such unrest in his long legs, which writhe from crooked to straight under the bedclothes. Sitting here on the covers we seem to be pinning him to earth, preventing him from hurtling towards extinction. As though for him there's only this torment or complete annihilation: no gentle, temperate resting place in between. I might have seen it from his point of view if he hadn't claimed to see it from mine: You'd have been better off without me, he declares.

That sets me off, of course. His better-off-without-me routine always does. Now I'm the one who's crying and shaking my head, even though there's this stranger, sitting there, staring. And then, can you credit it, the bitch starts trying to comfort me, to offer me advice as though she were a teacher or a mother.

Perhaps you would be better off, dear. Have you thought of that? But that's not the point, really, is it? The point is, people's lives are their own. I knew what your father was planning to do; he told me in advance. It made me very sad, of course, but I didn't think I had any right to try to stop him. He rang me from the office to say goodbye. Sometimes we have to show our love by letting go.

I'd let her go, if I could, from a very great height. In a way her little homily does the trick: my tears freeze on my face. She knew! He rang her! How can she sit there and tell this to me, his child? It's women like her who've induced his self-hatred in the first place. She's known him for what – a few months? She's not even pretty. Well, not particularly, not by my father's standards. She's realized he's never going to belong to her, she can't get him to live with her. So she'd as soon he died as went on living with us. Her desire to be special to him is so desperate now, she'd settle for being the last to say goodbye. I don't deign to answer her, I don't even take her comments into account. Does she think, just because I'm young, that my mind is open? That the prejudice against her runs more blindly in my mother's blood than in mine?

But my father is moved: he's prepared to give credence to this person, while my mother waits, discredited, out in the hall. He looks from his mistress's face to mine and back again, as though he's finding some innate likeness there: can't he see that my eyes are blue where hers are brown? He says, Will you do something for me?

He's weeping more copiously than ever. What else can we do but nod? We're subject to his weakness, like courtiers to a sickly king, whose whim, however fanciful, must be humoured. He says, and it seems such a little thing, I want you two to be friends.

She holds out her hand; I take it. Such things can be done. Her hand is just a hand, five fingers, a damp palm; is mine normal to her? Can the poison of enmity, when it courses through the veins, stop short at the wrist? She seems to survive. (Although she was to fade out of the story soon after, when my father got better and came home.)

My father relaxes his legs and closes his eyes; tears continue to seep sideways from under his lids. I wish him sleep more fervently than I wish him conscious-ness, but in the face of his tiredness I'm left with the terrible energy of my bafflement, which makes me want to fall to my knees beside him and shake him awake and force him to tell me, please, what is the *matter*? What have we done, my mother and sisters and I, what have we not done, that has made life with us unworthy to be lived?

I disengage my hand and get to my feet. He's asleep – I think I'll go now, I say, hoping to set an example to other visitors. But she won't budge, she's determined to outstay all comers, to be last to say goodbye all over again. I had wanted to elicit a message to take back to my mother, but it's clear I'm going to have to make one up. I run my palm along all the germy bed-rails I can lay my hands on, on my way out of the ward, in the hope of killing off one contamination with another. The accumulated breath of old men has worked its way deep into my lungs: I'm breathing it out now instead of in; when I see my mother and sisters I start to choke, and rush past them, out of the building, into the fresh air.

What did he say? they ask, when they catch me up. I'm wiping my hand compulsively on my skirt: I don't want to pass on anything nasty to them. My little sister's eyes are wide and impressionable – I'll have to edit out the mistress, for a start.

He didn't talk much, I say, looking cautiously at my mother. Her expression is fixed, impenetrable, strangely hard. She knows I'm lying, knows I have to lie. I prefer to address my remarks to my elder sister. He's a bit depressed, I say, but I think it's just drugs. He sends his love, and hopes they'll let him come home soon.

You were gone a long time, says my little sister suspiciously. She's at an age when life is just one long wait.

Well, I stayed with him, I say, until he dropped off to sleep. I look to my mother for confirmation that this was right, that this was what she would have done if she'd been there.

But she won't reassure me. Her eyes are devoid of the blessing I so sorely crave. And I can see that I can tell her about her rival or not: it will make no difference. Because when I sat on my father's bed in her place, I was that woman, myself.

## 19

Where's Daddy? says Mary: her eyes are wide and impressionable. She's just come in from school, and is used to seeing her father sitting at the kitchen table, drinking tea. The dogs, slumped against the wide refectory leg where his feet should be, rise up and revolve and slump again at the mention of his name.

I play deaf, opening a few unnecessary cupboards, getting out mugs for people who are never going to drink from them. There's tea in the pot and the usual number of buns in the oven: I'm hoping Mary's senses will capitulate to the normality of such smells.

But she says: Where's *Daddy*? again; she's getting quite cross. She's got something in her school bag that it's really quite imperative she should show him. I'm prepared to be shown instead, but she gives me one of her looks. It's something involving measurements, calculations; how could I be of any use? Her confidence, her frown, the way she's rummaging in her bag, are things that have an astonishing power to hurt me. It takes me a moment to work out why, although of course it's perfectly simple: she reminds me irresistibly of her father. He can get away from me, but I can't get away from him. He's here in the thunder of his nine-year-old daughter's brow, and worrying away at my ankles in the form of his baby.

Because Edith, at floor level, is racketing about on the tiles, flirting with danger, seeing if she can find a live socket to push her sucked, wet fingers into, a dog's open jaw to place her head inside. I get muddled between the rough physical handling essential for her safety, and the delicate emotional manoeuvring required for Mary.

He's gone! I shout brutally at Mary, as I gather up Edith and rock her wickedness, like sorrow, against my breast.

Gone? says Mary, as if in mortal need of a dictionary, as if despite her precocious way with language these four letters have finally got her stumped. I've seen that stupid expression before, in a dream. But I was never the one in the dream to wipe it away. And yet I can't stand it on her face for a moment longer. Gone up to London, I could say. Gone to take some work into the newspaper. Gone to have dinner with his editor. Might stay for breakfast with his agent. There are plenty of things I could say that would ease her mind. But I take a deep breath and break her heart. Gone to live with someone else, I say.

Edith squirms and laughs and claps her hand over my mouth. Mary has a way of registering things in slow motion: her cheeks tighten; the pupils of her large, moist eyes dilate, blackening their blue. Grief comes over her like some secret shame she's suddenly admitting to, creeps into her milky, English, child's skin like a blush. I ought to put my arms round her, I suppose, but

I can't, I'm already holding Edith. And God forbid that Mary should put her arms round me. It's just the sort of thing the soft-hearted little girl might do, and then anything might happen – I might become her child, and expect her to nurse me against her unformed chest like a baby.

Gone to live with who? says Mary. It's hardly the moment to start correcting her grammar.

A woman, I say tritely (I still can't say her name). Someone he's fallen in love with.

But Mary doesn't care what she's called. Her question is specific to her suffering. Does she have any children? she asks.

One.

A boy or a girl?

This is an emancipated, egalitarian child, but pain when it strikes is nothing if not chauvinistic. I can't work out which will hurt her more, someone prettier or someone with a train set. I'm stuck with the little matter of the truth. A boy, I say; a year or two older than you are.

She pauses, then says, What's his name?

So it comes down to that for her, too, in the end.

Ben, I say; and I see them falling down all over the world, all the Bens she's ever going to stumble across in her life. Benjamins, Benedicts, they all go at once, topple from her estimation before she's met them. She's nine, and already there's this category of really perfectly serviceably christened persons that she's never going to be able to make love to, or work with, or call a child after, or read about in a book. Ben, she repeats, starting

84

to hate the one she already knows at school who always wants to sit next to her at lunch-time.

I put down the baby and pour the tea. I'm glad that Mary's anger has been deflected away from her father. But she leaves her bun and refuses to drink her drink: it seems that the person she's angry with is me.

How long have you known about this? she asks.

Not, how long has her father been fucking someone else. How long have I, her mother, known about it.

A few months, I say. I tried to get over it. And he tried to give her up, but it didn't work out.

The colour is high on her neck now as well as her face. You pretended! she says, indeed, shouts – she's started to cry. You tried to make me think it was perfect. Why did you treat me like a baby? Did you think I was too young to understand?

Edith starts to copy her subversive tone, knocks over her mug and sends mouthfuls of bun flying into the air. Stay! I shout, afraid the dogs will start wolfing down the broken china, but they're sulking too and make no move to hoover up the mess. Frank designed this kitchen, the slate tiles, the lighting; we rubbed beeswax into this panelled wood together. And it *was* perfect, it *was*, I want to shout at Mary, before all this mess started spilling all over the floor. When I was her age, all I wanted was to be allowed to know nothing. But my Mary doesn't seem to be interested in the perks of being a child. What she wants is to be treated like an adult. Well, she can change Edith's nappy and clean up this kitchen for a start. I don't think I'll bother to get up from the table for a while.

For I can feel it now, my blood's propensity for

idleness coming over me. The only way to stop minding is to cease to care. Let the fridge ice over, let detritus encroach from the walls. If the dogs want the spat-out bun, let them eat broken china; let Edith crawl over their corpses, give her something to cry about. What's a happy childhood anyway, but an extended delusion? There are two kinds of mother, and I shall be the other kind, now.

## 20

The father of my best friend, Jill, is a judge. I'm only
eleven; I've never seen him in his wig. If I did I might
start laughing, not that he'd mind: I'm sure he'd agree
that he looked more like a pantomime dame in it than a
person empowered to pass sentence. If he were to
speak gravely to me, I'd think he must be kidding; I've
never seen him be the slightest bit grave with his own
children. Jill says whatever she likes to him, so I do, too,
but there's not the sense of risk that there is with my
own father, of treading on the tail of a tiger, who might
or might not turn round and bite your head off.

At Jill's place I feel extraordinarily safe: on the side of
law and order. Sitting at the judge's table, I am not with
the judged. There's none of the usual guilt I feel at
living in a grander house than my friends. Nancy, for
instance, lives in a tiny flat above a newsagent's: she
shares a bedroom with her sister and baby brother. I
hate her to see that we keep whole rooms empty except
for piles of old newspapers. Don't go in there, Nancy, I
say, let's go outside; but that's just as bad, since where
she just has street, we, at the moment, have this strange
steep rock garden, tier upon grand tier of it, rising up

for about a hundred feet from the road. I try to explain to her how useless it is, you can't play in it, our dog left home from exhaustion, but she's completely awed by it, has fantasies about making caves. The judge's garden has proper grass instead of stone paths, and trees and flowers, not prickly old cactuses and shrubs; but the real joy of it is, it's flat, it goes all the way round the house and back again, and that sets me free, that sends me running round in circles. I'm much more at home here than I am in my own house; I can bear all this privilege when it doesn't reflect on me. Besides, everything in Jill's house is so beautifully dusted. You pick up an ornament and it doesn't come coated in the accumulated grot of old grandmothers. Everything in my house is slightly cracked or ruined. You pick up an ornament and what comes off on your fingers is the fall-out from the atmosphere that is between my mother and father: her depression, his mania have settled over our possessions like a toxic deposit.

But in Jill's house everything is bright and clean and cared for. Although I doubt, somehow, if it's her mother who keeps it that way. She's always going off on the judge's arm to the opera or the ballet in full-length, off-the-shoulder shantung. I expect they have a maid who comes in and does the dirty work, including the ironing of all those strapless dresses. We've had maids too, in our time, but they've always been too busy being sacked or seduced by my father to get to know the house very well. And anyway, my mother won't let certain rooms be done. She says she wants to do them first herself.

Although Jill's house is dusted, it's not unduly neat:

there are things lying loosely around. But nothing to cause a hazard, no piles of paper to clamber over, no doors that won't quite open because of what's stacked behind. Everything runs smoothly: there's no threat from the environment, no constant fear that the chimney might catch fire, or the cellar be found flooded with water.

Jill and I don't go to the same school any more. She goes to the private college I was taken away from. I know about her world but she doesn't know about mine. I come to her now with the street glamour that state-school children once had for me. She doesn't know how apologetic I am in front of Nancy. She's too busy being apologetic in front of me. She feels the need to say sorry for her great good luck in life: the beam of satisfaction in her father's eye, the pampered gleam of her mother's bared shoulders. I'm not *always* allowed to have a midnight feast, she says. It's just that Mummy and Daddy are going out.

But her mother and father go out every time I come to stay. And Jill and I sit up gossiping and giggling and making crumbs in our beds. Nobody comes to shout at us. Nobody comes to protect us from the person shouting at us. And the food we wolf, full as we still are from dinner, comes fresh from the shelves of a recently defrosted fridge. I'm not responsible for the taste of it. I'm not responsible for anything except my own nocturnal capacity for fun and feasting. Jill throws her head back when she laughs: there are no fillings in her teeth, despite the shameless residue of chocolate biscuits which she certainly won't bother to get up and hygienically brush away. Nothing has seriously pained her, no nasty whining drill has broken through the enamelled surface of her confidence. There is a sheen on her of unblighted childhood that I, as her contemporary, cannot but bask in; when I am with her, I feel that shininess myself. My cheeks become rosy, I throw back my head when I laugh. The pain I feel for my mother at my father's infidelities falls from me, need not necessarily be mine. I feel in myself the potential to be another sort of girl altogether, a faithless girl, who tells stories to make people stare; who would turn her family into caricatures and their lives into anecdotes to make the party last till morning.

And even at breakfast it goes on (although Sunday breakfast at Jill's happens at lunch-time). Jill wants to share my jokes with her parents. And so, in the myth, my mother's sadness turns into madness: we don't go into *why* she's too distracted to defrost the fridge. Tell them about your father nearly drowning, says Jill. The one about the sharks and the bees. And I duly plant the image in a judge's mind of my father's body hanging from a tree.

And as a result of my faithlessness they love me. Of all Jill's friends, I am their undisputed favourite: they adore their family talent for drawing me out. I stir their compassion with my badly ironed dresses, my waiflike greed for their fried eggs and bacon. And I grow healthier in their company, like someone browning in the sun and beginning to sport bleached stripes in her hair. A great relaxation comes over me – happiness, I suppose – which I would not want my family to notice.

Wait for me in the car, I've begged my father in advance, and for once he actually follows my instructions. But the judge and his wife come out into the street to see me off. My father leaps from the driver's seat and doffs his hat. And the gesture, usually so dashing, so flattering, strikes me, to my horror, as deferential. For one thing, he looks better in the hat than out of it. What I have always regarded as his high, brainy forehead is maybe just an ordinary receding hairline. And his suit is too formal for such sunshine.

Hatless, in shorts, exposing his hairy head and knees, the judge is at some profound physical advantage. My father towers over him as he does over everyone, but next to the judge's thick-set rootedness, his height seems to make him sway unreliably. There's something ghostly about him, something already not quite with us, whereas the judge is reassuringly of this world. Despite the time he spends in chambers, the judge's complexion is ruddy; my father's pallor is of a person shut away from the light. I'm aware that he works too hard, that he has been working today, a summer's day, a Sunday. I take his hand. I do this not so much from allegiance as to steady him: after all, the judge's wife has her yellow hair piled up and is baring not just her shoulders, but her midriff. For all her fleshy curves and cultivated suntan, her beauty isn't serious like my mother's (or so I imply, with the pressure of my hand).

But he doesn't flirt with her. Strangely – almost, it seems to me, unkindly – he withholds from her the benefit of his charm. In fact he hardly notices her at all, so busy is he eyeing the judge with what transmits itself to me as abject nervousness. A pulse throbs visibly in his temple. His smile is too wide, and has got stuck. As witnesses go, I'm now completely discredited: this is nothing like the man I was describing at breakfast, yelping with bee-stung laughter above the jaws of sharks. I want to begin again, arrange things differently: have him come to the door, raise his hat in the old way, give Jill's mother one of his looks. But he and the judge have already embarked on a fateful conversation, the upshot of which is that our two families must get together.

What – all round to my place for cold lamb and tomato sandwiches? Or is he suggesting we come here? My mother could wear one of *her* hats: I'm sure she's got just the thing among her moth-eaten creations. As for visiting attire for my sisters – I'd be ironing all day. And all to throw my father back into this strange, diminished state, like a prisoner brought before the bench.

On the way home in the car, just to even up the score, I say some disloyal things about Jill's family. You don't have to lie, you just exaggerate the truth until what moves you becomes something to laugh at. And my father laughs loudly, and drives unlawfully fast; he likes me in my faithless vein as well. We make a pact, my father and I, to stave off this invitation, this get-together with the big-wig judge and his glamour-puss wife. They're too social for my mother, we make that our excuse, and Jill's getting a bit too much of a princess for me. What with her being an only child and filthy rich to boot, she's got her limitations as a friend.

So I spend my time with Nancy, who is certainly far from spoilt, but how I miss my darling Jill and her haughty ways. And when at last, months later, an invitation comes, I don't care who wears what, so long as I see her.

The invitation is to Bonfire Night. It isn't an occasion my family has cause to celebrate. The only bonfire I can remember is the one my father lit in the drawing room of one of our previous houses, in this, a country too hot to be bothered with the sweeping of chimneys. Assaulted by a stray pile of newspapers, he had begun screwing up the pages and systematically setting them alight. His temper was blazing, but although we children were in floods of tears, my mother stood dry-eyed and impenitent as he hurled her hoarded treasures at the flames. A smell worse than smoke filled the room: of roasting baby mice and birds. The maid of the moment came rushing in to announce that the chimney was on fire. My father took time off from hurling to ring the fire brigade: his voice on the phone had a reason-ableness that took my breath away. But although he resumed his temper, the fire calmed down; however many papers he piled on after that, the flames no longer leapt at his will from the chimney. He didn't ring to cancel. He let the fire engine come, with six men in helmets riding on the platform. I think he meant to excite us, it was his way of being a father, of lighting up our lives with his reckless ways. The firemen were sporting, they gave us a go with their hoses. They didn't seem to mind the waste of water or their time; they were men, after all, like my father, but susceptible to my mother: they ended up in the kitchen drinking her tea. And I remember how safe I felt then, as I stirred in their milk and two sugars, and one of them lifted me jovially on to his lap; as though the world were full of fathers who would not necessarily be angry, who would come when I called and not mind if my fears were unfounded. But eventually they went off, giving us one last listen to their brass bell, and my sisters and I were alone with our mother and father. And I dreamt that night we were dying, but not, strangely enough, from burning; what was killing us was a great, gushing torrent of water.

Fireworks in the fifties were on Empire Night. What greater cause for celebration could there be in the dominions than the birthday of our twelve-thousand-miles-away monarch? They had to pick cold weather in case of bush fires, so luckily it's coats all round. We're not the only ones to be invited. Jill has best friends other than me. In fact the lawn outside her house is teeming with them, all with their parents and brothers and sisters in tow. Most of the families know each other a little from speech days at my old private school. But no one in my family knows anyone. My little sister won't let go of my big sister's hand; her eyes are huge in anticipation of bangs. Where's Jill? I ask from time to time, but nobody knows where she's got to. I want to go inside the house and look for her. But I feel I must stay here and make sure there's such a thing as a soft drink for my mother. Won't you even have a Pimms? Jill's mother's husky voice keeps on saying. Some dry sherry perhaps? Or how about a little Campari soda?

My father is having no such problem. He's already downed two beers with his friend the judge. As far as their disparate heights make it physically possible, they've started thumping each other encouragingly on the back. Well, says the judge, licking the foam from his upper lip, we'd better get this damned show on the road. Will you do the honours for us, Jim?

My father is full of eagerness at being trusted. The fireworks lie in a great mound on the grass. Everyone here has contributed, and what with all these well-heeled fathers, keen to do Princess Jill proud, not to mention Her new young Majesty, Queen Elizabeth, there's every kind of pyrotechnic you could imagine, everything Brocks ever dreamed of; hour upon bright hour of fun. And of all the fond dads present here tonight, mine is to light the first touch-paper.

He understands the importance of getting it right. He's a businessman: he knows how these things should be handled. Nothing too showy at first to pre-empt the climax. But nothing too wimpish either – things should start with a bang. After a long and careful look he chooses a racy little jumping jack. And then backs across the lawn, clearing his throat to clear a path behind him.

Some stout devil's advocate of a father happens to have a box of matches to hand. My father takes them, bends down, strikes, steps back: all eyes are upon him. My big sister claps her hands over my little sister's ears. The touch-paper fizzes.

Like a manic grasshopper, the jumping jack leaps across the lawn. Its path is perverse: here, there, you can't predict it. You can't avoid it either: people rear back, but it jumps on, it's got such life in it, such elevation, such range. My little sister is crying and some children are already screaming before it even reaches its goal. It is going to end up in the middle of the pile of fireworks. Daddy! I shout, but it's too late. They're all going to go, the whole damned show, at once.

And really the thesaurus needs no serious editing, so here goes.

Luminary, illuminant, light, naked light, flame, fire, source of light, orb of day, orb of night, starlight, star, bright star, first magnitude star, Sirius, Vega, Aldebaran, Betelgeuse, Canopus, Alpha Centauri; evening star, Hesperus, Vesper, Venus; morning star, Phosphorus, Lucifer; shooting-star, fireball, meteor, galaxy, Milky Way, zodiacal light, gegenschein, aurora, northern lights, heavens, fulguration, lightning, sheet lightning, fork lightning, flash, levin, scintilla, spark, sparkle, flash; glow worm, lampyrine, firefly, firebeetle; noctiluca; fata morgana, ignis fatuus, will-o'-the-wisp, friar's lantern, Jack-o'-lantern, fire ball, St Elmo's fire, corposant, corpse-candle, deadlight, death-fire, death-flame, fire drake, fiery dragon; torch, brand, ember; torchlight, link, flambeau, wick, dip, farthing dip, rush, rush-light, naked light, flare, burner; lamp, lamplight, lanthorn, glim, bull's-eye, incandescent light, torch, flash-light, searchlight, arc light, flash-bulb, photo-flood, electric lamp, vapour light, neon light, magic lantern; chandelier, candelabra, girandole, son et lumière, limelight, spotlight, footlight; signal light, warning light, red, green, amber light; rocket, star shell, parachute light, flare, beacon, bale fire; lightship, sky rocket, Roman candle, Catherine wheel, sparkler, fizzgig; thunderflash; explosive, Greek fire, Bengal light; luminescent, incandescent, shining; lampyrine, lampyrid; phosphoric, fluorescent, radiant, radiating; colourful; bright, gay, light up, shine, make bright . . .

Oh yes, he made bright, did my father. And then there was the din of it as well.

Knock, knock-knocking, burst of sound, loud report, slam, clap, thunderclap, burst, shell-burst . . . but my hand is tired, as is indeed my spirit. And no list of words, however exhaustive, can convey the extraordinary synchronism of something that is all over in the time it takes to look up the word bang. Suffice it to say that the show was well and truly off the road. Out of sight, up the creek, dead in a ditch. We're five minutes into Jill's party and it's already over. And my father's face is something to behold. It's not just that he's let down Jill, or for that matter the Queen of England. It's that he's proved to himself that when it came to it he couldn't be trusted. He's known all along he was capable of this terrible conflagration. And through the smokescreen of his shame I catch a whiff of his mad, secret triumph.

And then at last I spot Jill, who has come out on to the balcony for the festivities. She's over by the house, high up, surrounded by friends.

Her head is thrown back.

She's laughing. I want to go home.

## 21

The nights are the worst. After Frank leaves, I can't get used to sleeping alone. It isn't just the bodily comfort I miss, his smell, the crook of his arm. What I miss is the concession I used to make to him in my dreams. Even in my sleep his presence placed a limit on the darkness; listening to him breathe I couldn't hear the silence beyond. Now that I can, I'm terrified. I don't dare let my hands touch my body. The poverty of it, the sadness of laying hands on myself when somewhere in the night he has his arms around her, might be too much too bear. I might start to rub open the rancid, sticky wound of my jealousy, I might find myself pornographically aroused by the image of my husband making love to another woman; I might start writhing to the rhythm of their contortions, trembling to the onset of their crisis until, with that strange rush of pricking warmth to the backs of my eyeballs that convinces me it can indeed send you blind, I might come to the theme of his body pumping spunk into hers. And then what a cry might escape me: what an abject, histrionic, deep-throated convulsion of surrender, such as a man might try to excite in a woman, and then draw back in horror at what he had unleashed. A noise like that in the night could scare the wits out of my children, they might wake up screaming and have trouble ever getting back to sleep again. So I try not to let my hands touch my body. Although I wake to find them clamped between my thighs.

Worse than the nights are the days. For one thing they're so long. They start at about 5 a.m., which is a bit early for a drink. At dawn the temptation to pick up the telephone is at its strongest. Quick, quick, I could say, fiddling with a box of matches, your house is on fire, come quickly. Or, turning on the taps: I'm afraid there's been a flood in the cellar. Or: Help, Edith's choking, she's got something stuck, I'm holding her upside-down, but she's turning blue. Or: Mary's in trouble at school, some sort of incident in the playground; the headmistress particularly asked to see the father.

I did ring once, and got Her. Hello, she said, who is it?

I honestly didn't know who, from her point of view, it could be. I couldn't say my name, it was the same as hers. Hello, she said again, who *is* it, please?

That please was not pleading but peremptory. I must have woken her but there was nothing remotely languorous about her tone. The word that most nearly describes it is brisk. My husband has left me for a woman whose quality is briskness. Who will leap out of bed when I hang up and do her early morning exercises.

Who *is* it? she says, for the third and last time: I'm holding her up with my silence, my inability to say your lover's wife, keeping her from getting her head down, or her leg over, or whatever activity she's currently finding so pressing. For now Frank comes on the line, it's his voice saying hello.

It's a voice I know in my bones. And I'm afraid my bones will answer for me, rattle out some awful female litany: Oh darling, it's you, thank God, come home, I need you. The struggle not to speak makes me breathe hard. So *that* is what the dirty callers are doing when they huff and puff at you audibly down the line: they're not just trying to convince you that they're *there*, or doing something strenuous with their free hand – they're trying their level best to protect you from their patter, which is twice as disgusting to them as it is to you. So, don't be afraid; it's the breather who is trembling; who regards you, the ear-piece, with a hushed and reverential awe.

Does Frank know it's me? Surely he must recognize my brand of muteness as it travels down the telephone wire which presently trails across his mistress's breasts. Or are there other lonely housewives who might bother him at this ungodly hour? Am I already so far from his conscience that he does not even suspect it might be me? His briskness, borrowed from her, would suggest so. How *busy* these sleeping people sound. Who is it, for God's sake? he says, and I slam the receiver down. Who for God's sake does he think? But I forget. I'm not the first. I am his second wife, who lay with him while tiresome phone calls came, wrong numbers, too trivial to trouble me mid-fuck – oh sod it, who can that be, ringing us *now*?

I can quite see I am extraneous to their plans, but I am here, and must be accommodated somehow. Loneliness is not just the longing for someone else, it's the embarrassment of finding yourself suddenly in your own company. What am I to do with me, this sad, heavy creature who hasn't even got the grace to go to sleep, but is full of a dismaying, clumsy energy too unfocused to line up with any degree of efficiency behind a hoover or a garden spade? I'm hardly a fit companion for my children; one look at me in my present mood and they throw psychosomatic temperatures or come out in undiagnosable spots. I can't concentrate to read a book: my own banal story seems to me so much more compelling. But to whom can I tell it? Not the public at large, for a start, which puts paid to my writing, the thing I'm supposed to labour at, my job. My mind doesn't flood with poetry at being left. It floods instead with some pretty predictable and humourless generalities which God forbid should leak their way on to the page.

So, in the easy decadence of my middle-class existence, I call in a baby-sitter and drive myself up to London to see a friend. I have it in mind to cry on her shoulder and sink half a bottle of her scotch. It's not something I've done much of, opening up my heart to other women, and I'm not sure if it's particularly advisable. But it's what women do, so I suppose I'd better give it a try.

I thought I'd feel more outgoing when I got out of the house, but the route shocks me, it's the one Frank took every time he drove up to town to see That Woman, and there's no road sign or petrol station that doesn't refuel my pain and redirect it back towards myself. Normally a dogged, slow-lane driver, I'm bowling along at ninety, overtaking anything that comes within my sights. But danger will not be courted: the worst that happens is that I arrive half an hour early to see my friend.

So I take a detour round Shepherd's Bush, which is where Frank is living with his new lady. It's a sweat to find her house: it's in a back street, a dead end behind a busy, ugly high road. I've been left not just for an older woman but for a humbler one. Of course it's a perfectly smart terraced house by London standards; after all, she's a professional high-flier despite being a one-parent family – up till now. But after his studios and his acres where will Frank put himself? (Don't ask.) I've imagined she's playing some game with me, but she's been dealing cards from an entirely different pack. Her trump of course is sex, but it's more dangerous than that. My gentle country fields lose potency against the abrasive meanness of these streets, and it comes to me sinkingly that I am a city girl who has somehow got herself fatally out of context. There's a newsagent on the corner, and for some reason I expect Frank to appear at any moment in trainers (he never wore such footwear at home) and go running (he never ran) down there to collect the papers (at home they always plopped through the door). But here there will be an itinerant charm in fetching them plus some extra squalid rag he'd normally refuse to have in the house.

His sports car sits outside number thirty-six. (*Her* age – I'm nowhere near that yet.) Even though he hasn't been through the car wash once since he left home, I'm surprised someone hasn't put a brick through his elegant windscreen. I'm not tempted to myself. I've sunk down in the seat of my sedan; I'm as faint-hearted a watcher as I am a breather. I can't raise my eyes to the windows of number thirty-six. Her house is like a person I can't quite look in the face, with its terraced tongue in the cheek of the next-door porch. Its heavily veiled eyes (Frank hates curtains) hide inner eyes – his, hers, her son's – and all I want is to escape their triple gaze, but I'm facing the wrong way up a no-through road having lost the capacity to execute a three-point turn. I attempt a nine-point one instead, knocking over a dustbin in the process, and end up backing down the street, all my gears grinding, cats leaping from my path. And as I join the angry traffic and am away, I'm jubilant for a second until I remember that Frank is the person I'm used to escaping *towards*.

Still, I have a destination of sorts. I've chosen Nina carefully as being the most self-absorbed of my friends and therefore the least likely to feed off my misery. Also, she's as fond of Frank as she is of me. I plan to be as vile as I like about him, but woe betide anyone who dares take my part against his. But her main qualification is, she's at home. She's an actress, so you can rely on her not to be busy.

Nina lives in a mews house in Kensington. You go up some stairs beside a dirty old garage to find yourself in conditions of startling splendour. Nina's pretty splendid herself: beautiful in a way I admire but don't usually envy, since it's the way that takes time and costs money. But today the priority she gives it and the particular russet-gold tinge she's achieved with her hair seem calculated in some way to hurt my feelings. What's more, the abstracted look on her face makes me wish I had picked on one of my more motherly friends. But I must be disloyal to Frank in all loyalty to myself, and Nina seems to understand what I'm here for. She draws me solicitously into the kitchen. So tell me, Roz, she says, how *are* things?

I take a deep breath.

But before I can let it out she's telling *me*.

Oh Roz, she says, Roz, I just have to talk to someone. And wouldn't you know it, she's crying on *my* shoulder.

She's in love, so it seems, with someone other than her husband. Oh Roz, she says, Roz, you don't know, you can't possibly imagine. Of course I love Hugh (that's her husband). He's the father of my children. But I have never, *never*, experienced such . . . such . . .

The word turns out to be tenderness. I've heard of extra-marital sex, but extra-marital tenderness takes some adjusting to. It hints at something more serious than fucking, some messy, maudlin, latent merging of mouths; it forces me to re-evaluate the athletic image of Frank and That Woman in my mind and picture them lying quietly in each other's arms while the germ of sentiment spreads like an infection between them.

Does Hugh know? I ask; Nina stares at me distractedly. The truth is, she's hardly thought about it. Perhaps, she says. Or perhaps he doesn't want to find out. Or has some vested interest in not discussing it. *That* would be a relief, she says, if he had someone else of his own.

How far from civilized my behaviour has been all this while! How could I have been so crass as to have failed to provide a fourth party?

Wouldn't you be jealous? I say lamely, but she's impatient with the subject, ruthless in her desire for me to concentrate my mind on her lover. His passing gentleness. His little cruelties. What he said, what he wrote, what he whispered. She wants to lay these things before me in merciless detail so that I can judge from the evidence whether or not he loves her. He has a wife of his own, but that's not the problem, there's no reason to be jealous of *her*, Nina assures me. The wretched woman's pathetic, keeps ringing up at all hours; has even stooped to using the children to blackmail him. Once, when Nina was visiting his new flat, the poor obsessive creature parked outside in her car and just sat there. No, the problem is Nina herself, her inability to trust, to believe that this god among men can really want her.

I don't know why she has to hear that he does from me. She's heard it often enough from him, by the sound of it. Nor do I understand what kind of proof she's looking for. He *makes* love to her, doesn't he? I have all the proof I need that Frank no longer wants me. But she's anxious that I should be clear in my mind what it is, this being in love. While I busy myself about her kitchen, getting us coffee, she sits on the kitchen table, dangling her waxed legs and smoking. He *moves* me, you see, she explains as I grind the black beans. We *delight* in each other, she points out as I scalp the warm milk.

We adjourn to the bedroom with our mugs while she gets ready to go out. I had thought we might have lunch, but she's arranged to meet her new man in a restaurant. Isn't she afraid of being seen? She shrugs; if she's seen, she's seen. Such fears are obviously peripheral to the fear of the pain her lover has the power to cause her: will he be late, will she be dressed right, will he have to rush away? There is a purity of purpose about the way she makes her preparations which has its own disarming morality; as well as painting her toenails and putting on silk underwear she has to cover her tracks at this end with lying notes to her husband and the children's nanny, as well as leave them something to heat up, should she be late back. I follow her back into the kitchen and watch her knock up an expert lasagne, continually tasting it and licking her fingers, spreading her juices around with the profligacy of a woman desired by more than one man at once. She offers me bolognese sauce on some toast in case I'm hungry, catering for others effortlessly in her passion to please herself. Then back to the bedroom to put on what she calls her war paint: I'd thought she was made up, but apparently that was only an undercoat. I hope you don't mind, she says, but I said I was having lunch with you. That's all right, I say, and actually I mean it.

Because there is a boundless energy and diligence in her for these little betrayals; as an actress she is lit from within because she knows what she needs to know most: she knows what her action is, and her action is to meet her lover. The simplicity of it, the clarity, renders all her other actions sacrificial: no task is too sordid or humiliating to be tackled with ingenuity and joy.

Where will it lead? I ask.

Lead? she says. Lead? Well, to disaster, of course. I'll lose all this – my security, Hugh, my family. And him, too, when he finds out how easily he can have me.

But her eyes stay dry and bright, she's just done her

mascara. And the note that defies her trained tones is of exultation. Well, I say, I envy you, you're lucky.

Yes, she says, I am: you're a good friend, Roz. It's done me so much good to talk to you. I hope you'll let me cheer you up one day. Promise you'll turn to me when you're in trouble.

I promise. The lie, after all, is subsidiary to my action, which, now she's got her coat on, is to leave. But once outside, I'm without motivation. Directionless. I feel foolish in front of myself to drive straight home. I *could* go and see Frank's mother, who is dying slowly in a West London hospice. But Frank hasn't wanted to upset her by telling her we're separated: I'd have to call her Mother and say how much we're looking forward to having her home for Christmas. So I abandon my car instead on a double yellow line and do a bit of spending in the high street.

These new boutiques are no good to me – what I want is an old-fashioned department store where I can wander round among the lipsticks and the scents and the scarves and feel as women used to before they knew any better, that it's perfectly legitimate just to want to be *groomed* and decked about the neck with chains and fur. The mood I'm in, I might even buy a hat.

But the shop I find my way into doesn't have a millinery department. It doesn't have a beauty salon either. This is the seventies and grooming has come a long way: you're supposed to walk in here not just with pre-waxed legs, but with legs that never grew hairs on them in the first place. The look of the day is child-like; the salesgirls all have the same corrupted orphan face, painted blank white, with lipstick so dark it looks black in the simulated lamplight. They're dressed in shiny un-ironed garments like jumble-sale petticoats, through which you can see their deliberately undeveloped breasts. But fashion's magic prevails: I have a longing to look just like that. That dress you're wearing – where can I find one? I ask.

The girl I pick on looks at me resentfully, as though the merchandise here is not really meant for the public. On the fourth floor, I think I hear her mutter.

I take the lift, but it seems she's misdirected me. The famous old store has been taken over on all floors by bowls of giant, dyed feathers, waving like living things in the incense-breathing air. On the floor below I discover some rails of clothes in little caves, but they are for children. Ingenuous adults apparently have sophisticated offspring: these are slinky evening dresses for tiny-waisted two-year-olds with labels in the back that say dry clean. I pick out one for Edith to spill her breakfast down and then go in search of a bigger size for Mary in case she's jealous. The dress I find is hardly a viable alternative to jodhpurs, but I'm thrilled with the fabric, which is sprayed with silver stars. Trouble is, when it comes to paying there's no till. Nobody seems interested in my money. Where will I find my size? I ask. But some strange, whining, mesmeric music is being blared through speakers: no one is able or indeed inclined to hear.

I sail down a floor on an escalator with the dresses I've decided on tucked under my arm. Here, suddenly, are a hundred things to fit me: flowing skirts and clinging crêpey tops in shades of oyster and prune. The fitting room is communal and full of people falling over each other in the gloom. I try on more things than I brought in with me – some, I suspect, may be other customers' clothes. Nobody seems to mind. Nobody's interested in whether or not anything suits me. I find something in sludge-green that I covet but it doesn't have a price tag. How much is this? I ask. The salesgirls turn their blood-lipped faces away from me, into the many mirrors. I catch the down escalator with my prospective purchases held out over my arm, extended a little from my body for maximum visibility. Perhaps you're supposed to pay in one go on the ground floor. But the girl at the till looks up at me in annoyance. I can't take for those – this is blushers and body stockings, she says.

I drop the dresses on the floor and walk out of the shop. But a customer runs after me and stops me just outside the door. Here, she says kindly, you left these. And frankly I give up. Thanks, I mutter and clutch the wretched things to my chest. And then, as I proceed, I realize I'm walking quite jauntily, happy at the hand that I know is going to land on my shoulder.

But none does. The authorities refuse to apprehend me. They haven't even given me a parking ticket although I've been causing an obstruction for over an hour. I start sobbing at the sight of my empty windscreen. It's not that I'm expecting anyone to be *moved* by me, or to *delight* in me. But I think at the very least they might arrest me. People ought not to be allowed to get away with things – there have got to be rules. Because if I can take anything of anybody's, maybe nothing was ever mine.

## 22

We were used to our father leaving us. Sometimes, secretly, we felt better off without him. But it was different the time our mother left. When I was eight she sailed away on a ship. Ostensibly she was going on a trip to see my aunt, whose husband had been posted to Singapore. But of course what she was really doing was trying to turn the tables on my father, to be the one doing the leaving, just for once.

The effort it was costing her to go through with it was nearly killing her. She had four hat-boxes with her to give her strength. My father held our hands and tried to look reliable. Or at least he held hands with my two sisters. I was one more than he could manage, to my relief.

We went below, into my mother's cabin. It was the sort of place that in other circumstances would have entranced me. But it was full of friends and relations sitting all over the bunk beds and obscuring the port-hole, wishing my mother *bon voyage* and hoping to move in on my father. Here's to a happy holiday, they said, raising not only their glasses but their eyebrows, censorious at the sight of the hat-boxes, not to mention the champagne, which if they'd had a little less of themselves they might have noticed the holiday-girl wasn't touching. They thought it remiss of a mother to go gadding off abroad without her family. My mother's hat was helmet-shaped and her smile was so mettlesome it cut your heart, but they couldn't tell courage from callousness. My sisters flung their arms round her neck. I did no such thing: she was having trouble enough keeping her head. Aren't you going to kiss your mother goodbye? said some bosomy cousin, assuming the newly vacant job of minding my manners. I raised my face stiffly to be kissed. Since she must go, I wanted her gone quickly. I was anxious to get ashore. There was a sinister sick feeling in my stomach which I took to be a landlubber's fear of being left on board. Let's go, I kept saying rudely. Can't we go?

My sisters made up for my cold-heartedness by crying. Poor little girls, everyone thought as they shepherded us down the gang-plank. They were sorriest of all for my little sister, and she *was* a moving sight. Her eyes were huge and she clutched a bedraggled teddy bear.

But I was not convinced by my sister's suffering. Real unhappiness, the sort that sears the soul, is not huge-eyed. Nor does it clutch at bears. Unhappiness scowls, stands apart, will not take the offered hand. It does not cry because it knows it can never be comforted. It believes, it actually believes, that there is only one love. And it will not try to make do with any other.

My mother's aura left me like a ship moving slowly away from the dock. First, like a sheer white cliff, it overhung the wharf where we stood waving. And then creakily, sluggishly, but with the deep, sombre impetus of a force of nature, the separation began. I was joined to the ship's rail by a red paper streamer which was tougher and more tenacious than I expected: it grew tighter and tighter until for a moment I seemed to be pitted against the ship's full power, before it snapped, and sagged with the others into the harbour.

My mother's face, crammed in among the faceless crowds lining the deck, shone down on me at first with such extraordinarily dream-like particularity that it seemed to reflect like a moon in the widening water. But then the water was churned up, or her smile clouded over, or something; my memory of her blurred and broke up in front of my eyes. And I could no more will her image back to my mind than I could turn the ship round as it headed importantly out to sea.

I'm cold, said my younger sister plaintively, keen to leave, now that I wanted to stay. My father put his hat back on. Come on, Ro, said my older sister, who was mother now.

I wound in my streamer, wet and limp, with its red dye running. The colour came off upsettingly on my dress. I was cold with dread. Not just dread of going home alone with our father, or of which blonde he might wheel in to help with the washing. Dread that without my mother's eye on me I, too, would blur and break up into pieces. It had been in an effort to cheer her that I had always tried my hardest, done my best, bothered at all. Now, although she had sailed away, it was I who found myself in a strange country: that barren and dismal land beyond the favour of her soft, amused, indulgent, doting regard.

She came back of course. People who love you always do. But I was surprised when I saw her again how her face had changed. Or had grown less familiar to me. In some ways my image of her was clearer, as though I'd been looking at her before through some sort of veil. What I saw now was a good-looking but rather over-weight woman, whose smile sometimes struck me as hard. But then, perhaps in the interim I had lost my own ability to distinguish between callousness and courage.

And ten years later, when I sailed away myself, though I cried when I kissed her goodbye, I found that waving from the deck, your perspective is changed: you've got hold of the other end of the streamer. And this time when it snapped it didn't drop down with the others into the tangled papery mess littering the water; it was lifted up by the wind and what with the ship's gathering speed, it streamed out behind me like a banner.

## 23

Look, says Mary one Sunday. We've come back into Daddy's comic strip.

Sure enough, so we have. It's ages since Frank has been moved to depict us. In fact the piece has hardly warranted being called *The Blades* for months now, although it still features Harry Blade and his carryings-on at the office, in particular with a female television journalist in a safari suit, who reports pertinent things from the Lebanon. Now, suddenly, there's an abrupt change of material: here we have Mrs Blade and the two little Blades being bailed up at their front door by Harry, looking sheepish, with his two suitcases. The knock, knock, who's there caption is hardly more biting in context than it is out of it, but it strikes *me* as funny. Edith, who can't read yet, finds it pretty uproarious too. And from then on, Sunday after Sunday, Frank insinuates his way back into our laughter.

The joke is the one about the husband falling in love with his ex-wife. He's up to all the old ploys. Ringing her up at all hours of the night too tongue-tied to speak, although she says, Come on, I know that's you. Sitting outside her place in his car, hoping not to be noticed – a difficult feat in the case of our house, which is in its own grounds at the end of a long, lone drive. Also, the dogs are not fooled by his anonymity: they've got their paws up on his windows and are full of such violent welcome that the whole family comes rushing out to see what the fuss is. Since he's driven so far and the children are so thrilled to see him, it would be churlish of the wife not at least to ask him in for a drink. And pretty soon he's got his feet under the kitchen table, pinned down by the dogs, who are slumped one up against each leg . . .

In fact it was nowhere near so easy. For a start, one of the dogs had killed a sheep and had had to be put down. And although Frank wanted to come back, I didn't want to stay. Oh, I don't mean with him, but here where we lived, in the country. I insisted we put our beautiful house on the market. We needed the money, of course: Frank's new, morbid, cartoon style was no longer commanding the frivolous sums from syndication we were used to, and I was (still am) undiscovered as poets go. But I would have sold it anyway. Not *just* because I hated the local farmer who had personally shot my dog at point-blank range. Nor do I *think* I was trying to punish Frank. My reason was more urgent and more personal: I was afraid of being identified with property. In order to see if it was really me Frank wanted, I had to live in a more horrible house than Hers. Linda's: there, I could say it. From the new magnanimity of my reduced domestic circumstances I hoped to bring myself to use her name.

We moved back to London in early July. (We had moved into the country late one May. And if I wanted to define innocence, or hopefulness, I would instance the day when we put the smell of the city behind us – the dustmen were on strike as I remember – and arrived by way of the pale, unfurling beech woods to find the azaleas in full vulgar-scented bloom. The dogs were puppies and the cat was a kitten in those days, and though we filmed them romping photogenically in the tipped-out packing cases, off camera they were already patrolling the property, fouling its borders systematically with their secretions, electing sacred places in the woods for the bones of their kills. And Frank and Mary and I were as primitive as they were: we thought that happiness was a place you could exchange contracts on, and carpet, and stalk about in, in the conviction that what you were was what you had.)

Now, moving back to town, we are more circumspect. We refuse to be diminished by the fact that the rooms of our new house are so much smaller. We don't let bricks and mortar go to our heads, although it's difficult to stop the dust from the walls we've knocked through from clogging up our sinuses and inflaming our eyes. I congratulate myself on no longer being a school bus: there's a perfectly decent school just round the corner. And the dog seems to settle for a back garden after a few initial nights of disorientation, whining for the woods or his buried bones or the ghost of his lost brother.

The cat, I have to confess, was less adaptable. At first she simply refused to move at all. We were all packed to go: the removal men had set off, and we – family and animals – were to follow close behind. But although we called and called her affected name, Minouche, she would not come. We tried her more ordinary nicknames. Kitty, we called, and then more plainly, Puss. But she remained incognito. We were forced to file through the rooms we'd wanted to avoid revisiting: our voices bounced self-consciously off the pictureless walls. Oh Kitty, we cried, where are you? Not in the house apparently. So out into the garden we trooped (Mary by this time was sobbing) and continued our procession through purple passages of dying rhododendrons. Even Edith, who was too young to understand themes of lost innocence, or being expelled from Eden, could conceive well enough of the parable of the missing cat; indeed when she started school her compositions were to feature nothing but threatened kittens, kittens freezing, or perishing from hunger, or being eaten by wolves in the forest – her teachers would comment in the margin: Highly imaginative, Edith, but the subject was My Favourite Pastime.

In fact the cat turned up a few days later: the new people found her in the coal cellar when they arrived. I had to drive all the way back to the country to fetch her. Bumping down the pitted drive, the pit of my stomach was subject to unpredictable lurches of emotion; there is no loss so sickening as the loss of something you've given up of your own volition. The clematis and white wistaria were having a second flowering and the house was decked about like the kind of bride only a fool would have jilted. The new owners asked me in; they seemed keen to show me round what I so recently had been showing them. But I stuffed the cat in her basket and fled, and she yowled for both of us all the way back to London.

Despite the extravagant welcome we offered her –

disgusting steamed coley fish for God's sake – the cat continued to sulk. She, who had once been our familiar, now scorned our laps. Even Edith, whose creature warmth she had been keen to cuddle up to, to the extent of leaping into her pram and curling up on her face, was to be disdained. She took her tortoiseshell charms a few doors down the road and spent more and more time in the mouse-ridden house of a little old lady who was only ever to be seen wearing black. And when the old lady moved away, our cat went with her, and we finally had to acknowledge that relations were severed.

It seemed at first to be the same with Frank. He couldn't settle either. With or without seven acres of Berkshire, I was not enough for him. He'd fallen into the habit of yearning: put him with Roz, and all he wanted was Linda; let him have Lind, and Rosa was the only one. I had to learn to say more than just her name, I had to pick up the phone and say, Please help me, he's crying, he misses you, I think you'd better drive over here and get him. And then there would follow the times when he would steal away from her to see me, the times that I came to find perversely exciting, because he was doing with me at last what he'd done with her, pushing me on to the floor or across a table, or up against the wall, and pulling off my clothes and fucking me as though I were something forbidden. You will think I had no pride. But my pride was that I had none. And you must understand that I was afraid it might occur to him to kill himself. We talked about it once, and he swore he never would. But I had heard a man cry like that once before.

I don't know what I did during that time, other than

stand close to the window, with the curtains subtly parted like an unbuttoned skirt, and simply wait for him. God knows whether Edith was ever toilet-trained, or what Mary found in her sandwiches when she bit into them at school. It was my madness of course, but it seemed to me towards the end, as the motor of the thing ran down, that events began to speed up artificially, like a film shot on a slow-cranked camera, until he was leaving me and coming back on a daily basis, and our cries and dramatic gestures assumed a jerky, squeaky-voiced unreality, more comical, indeed farcical, than tragical. And who knows, it may have been laughter that saved us. Or just plain tiredness. For I don't think he struggled with himself morally and made a decision, or that she ran out of patience or clean sheets and kicked him out. I, certainly, did nothing so crass as to forgive him. It just seemed to me in the egocentricity of my pain that their affair was an illness I finally began to recover from. I didn't wake up one morning miraculously better. I just noticed I'd stopped noticing my symptoms. The fever that clouded my head had all but cleared. The constriction in the muscles of my chest became less weighty. The lump in my throat, past which I couldn't swallow, subsided. My appetite came back: Let me take you out to dinner, said Frank.

I walk into the restaurant with my old confidence: if we're seen, we're seen. When I say old, I mean the sort of confidence I used to have when Frank was married to his first wife. In those days I didn't fear confrontation, the public moment that negates all the private ones, when if we ran into Her (his first wife's name was Jean) he would have to turn this way or that, take her arm or mine, align himself irrevocably with one of us, to the eternal fury and sorrow of the other. Not that I had any expectations of being chosen at that time. But I could rely on my courtesan's manners to relinquish him kindly. What I came to fear as a wife was my own black wifely outrage that would see him torn in two, split clean down the middle, rather than have him walk away openly with my rival.

But now at our table for two I can eat quite heartily. The food doesn't seem sent to taunt me: nude pink prawns reclining frothily in a semen sauce. I'm not threatened by the candlelit faces ranged round the walls; no one here tonight has red-gold hair. There's a preponderance of brown, like mine, although mine now has white streaks. For a long time I tried to grow it long down my back like Linda's, but this morning, on a whim, I had it cut quite drastically short; when I'm prompted, as I often am, to run my fingers through it, I have the delightful and reassuring experience of not recognizing my head to be my own. Frank seems to enjoy the confusion, too: he keeps reaching rather rudely across the table to rub his palm over the shorn shape of my crown, as a mother might caress the skull of a newborn baby, coveting the bones that have caused her so much passion and pain. His words, like his touch, are full of a kind of rueful compulsion: You always knew, didn't you, he's saying, that you were the only one I ever really cared about; if it hadn't been for you I wouldn't have cared what became of me. And I believe him, although he's doubtless said such things to other women, his mistress, his first wife, possibly even

Mary; I know by the look on his face that what he says is true.

What's more, he's right, his declaration doesn't surprise me: it's as though I've seen it coming, heard it all before, I can't be disrupted by joy any more than I can be by sorrow. Back now, where I belong, in the gentle steady beam of Frank's affection, it's as hard to imagine feeling threatened as it is to sense what it's like to freeze or sweat when the weather's perfect. Frank smiles at me, and I smile back at him, and the gamey smell of the pheasant on my plate overtakes my senses more powerfully than love can. I am all bones at the moment and can wear my stolen sludge-green dress in the confidence that I have the corrupted orphan looks to go with it. But that won't last: being cared for will foster my old indifference; my waist will thicken, innocence will overtake me again, my natural state will turn out, after all, to be contentment. Frank's talking to me gallantly, suggesting we swap tastes of each other's sauces, but my eyes stray over his shoulder, as if on the look-out for something to spoil my appetite: some hungry people have come in and are being shown to a corner table; the first rush of adrenalin I've had all night accompanies the impression that Linda may turn out to be one of them.

But it isn't her. It's just another blonde with hennaed hair. And when we get home I realize there's no circumstance in which it could have been. Because when we turn on the television and flop down in front of it, full of pheasant, there she is on the late-night news, being transmitted to us, live, from Entebbe.

She's looking amazonian in a flying suit, unzipped to reveal a discreet amount of cleavage. There's the whirr of helicopter blades on the soundtrack and a glamorous Israeli commando on the sidelines whose opinion she's eliciting from time to time about events that are currently shaping all our destinies. I must admit you have to admire her style.

Frank, as always, has hold of the remote control, and I wait for him to flick her politely away, if not for my sake then at least for his, to spare himself the sight of such lithe and burning-eyed male zealotry looming so close to our woman in the jungle.

But nothing happens. She blathers on, to my intense fascination, and when I dare to turn round to see how he's reacting, I'm amazed to find he's fallen fast asleep. The food and the wine and the hour have got the better of him, and she can be as hard-hitting as she likes, she isn't reaching him now on any level. His head lolls loosely back on the sofa, its heaviness shifting subtly to my shoulder. His head is the part of him that holds what I have loved best in this world: his wit, his fraternity, his judgement; the weight of these things lies crushingly on my clavicle. With my untrapped hand I edge the control button out of his grasp and make her vanish, even from his dreams.

And sitting in front of the spluttering, abandoned screen, it comes to me that I will miss her more than he will. Something has gone on between this woman and me of which he, in his sleep, is childishly innocent. Messages have been passed back and forth between us which he has carried unwittingly, like brand marks on his body, despatches in braille for the tactile correspondent, kisses in code, caresses by courier from Rose to Linda and back again, safety and risk mad to taste each other, with their mouths pressed to his mouth where her mouth has been. And now the exchange is over. I'll never get to wear her flying suit. And with the slipstream from the helicopter still roughing up her hair, she must know she can never be pinned to the chair, like me.

## 24

I've never been close to death, myself. Although when I was five I was knocked down by a bicycle. It doesn't sound much, but as two-wheelers went the bike was big and fast. I, being small and weak, was laid out cold. The poor distraught cyclist lifted me up and carried me before him in his arms until a neighbour recognized me and directed him to our front door. I was handed, still unconscious, to my mother, who nearly fainted herself at the sight of me. That's all really. I came round, slightly concussed, but completely unharmed. The cyclist, not much more than a teenager, came in for a cup of tea. Nobody blamed him: I simply hadn't been noticing where I was going. I hadn't stopped at the kerb and looked right, left, and then right again before walking briskly across as I'd been taught to. I'd seen something I wanted on the other side of the road, and launched myself under the wheels of the oncoming rider.

What I'd seen, and this is what I'm getting at, were flowers. My earliest ambition in life was to be a florist, and to this end I collected what blooms came my way. The ones I was allowed to pick were wild, or poked through people's fences into the street: bartonia, spider

orchids, flannel flowers; nothing very bright or bounti-
ful. I was always crouched down to grass level, or suspended at hedge height, hurting my hands on thorny
twigs or stems that would not snap.

Then, coming home from school that fateful day, I
saw something gleaming. It might have been candollea,
or perhaps even laburnum (if the bike hadn't got me,
some poison surely would have done). But from my
point of view it was what I'd dreamed of. And after
the accident happened I went on dreaming. While I lay
apparently lifeless in the road, another vibrant part of
me rushed on, not letting the sickening thud interfere
with its obsession to fill its happy arms with golden
flowers.

From across the road I was aware of my body being
lifted, arms and legs and head pathetically dangling; I
was aware of the young man's fierce and breathless
contrition, the beat of his heart against my ribcage as he
ran; I heard the ring on the doorbell and my mother's
anguished voice calling to me wildly to come back to my
senses.

But I was loath to obey her. My senses were taken up
with other things, the smell of yellow, the taste of
petals, the smoothness of stems that broke bloodlessly
at my touch. What's more, I was in no pain. And the
only way back to consciousness was past the terrible
throbbing in the front of my head.

I opened my eyes, nevertheless. And it was worth it
to see the joy in their faces. It was, I suppose, now I
think of it, the first romantic moment of my life. But as
the warmth of my mother's arms closed round me I felt
the stifling of a different passion that was pulling me

towards cold oblivion. Where I would have gone perfectly gladly. Intent on flowers.

## 25

So. I'm twenty. A woman of the world. Well, seen a bit of it, anyway, although I'm back, now, where I started, living in Sydney. The story of my adult life so far is as follows: I've been to London, met Frank, fallen in love with him, taken fright at his wife and run home to my mother. Except that my mother isn't here. She and I have swapped sides of the globe. With my sisters in tow she's taking the opportunity to stay in my flat in London while I'm living in her house with my father. I ought to mention that my parents have split up; their marriage didn't survive my going away (I always feared it was my will that kept them together). My father now has a flat of his own, but since I've been home, and in my mother's absence, he's moved back into the family house as caretaker. To take care of me.

I don't take too kindly to his ministrations, as I've been living for two years in London completely unshepherded. But I'm a penniless student, so I'm not in a position to complain. I've taken up the place at university I scorned two years ago, and spend my time in lectures making notes on airmail paper for the thesis on love I'm submitting by correspondence to Frank.

My father and I rub along all right. Although I can see he has a fantasy about living with me that is different from what is actually taking place. It can't have escaped his notice that my real emotional intensity is for the postman. The fact is, I don't pay much attention to my father. He's fifty now, and isn't going to hit me. He likes things to be clean, but then these days, so do I: we have quite a lot of fun together throwing out old newspapers. To upset my mother, he's getting the whole house painted and wants to talk about colour schemes; he has a liking for white, with a dated dash of pink, or grey. Mmm, I say, yes, that'll be nice Dad. I care about the colour of walls passionately, but something in me refuses to be engaged. Is engaged elsewhere. Has an image of a man, not so tall, with more hair, with whom I'd like to be discussing matt emulsion.

Anyway, my father's not short of someone to sit at his feet. His secretary's on the phone every five minutes. And there's some other woman he's involved with: a marriage counsellor no less; he's often attracted to people in the helping professions. This one's married unhappily, a discredit to her profession, but that doesn't seem to have taught her to keep her counsel. Your father works too hard, she advises me a minute after we've met; he worries too much – he should spend more time relaxing with his friends. Meaning her, of course. She wants, as so many women have before her, to rock his troubles against her sainted breast. But he's in retreat from her attentions; using having to live here with me as an excuse for not letting her stay with him in his flat. I know this, but it doesn't make me triumphant. It would have done once. But winning, when it comes, is always too late. It's over now, the need to stand up (or was it in) for my mother, and keep my father faithful at all costs. Now all I feel is the weight of responsibility. And embarrassment at my role as proxy wife.

For the truth is, the woman's right about his state of mind. He *does* work too hard. Sometimes he can hardly eat his breakfast for worrying. He sits with the *Herald* open at the business section, reading the stocks and shares while his face changes from one white to another: first white with a dash of pink, and then of grey. All our lives he's been on the verge of bankruptcy. Yet we've always lived in glamorous houses like this one, which happens to have a verandah overlooking the harbour. I can only imagine he's dealing in such vast sums that the current roof over our heads is immaterial. Now that I'm grown up I know I should be pressing him to confide in me, getting him to tell me, please, what is the *matter*? But I don't. Not just because I hear the post-man coming up the path, or I have to rush to catch the ferry to college. I don't because I can't. And I can't because I am his child. We're alone here, you see. And I'm afraid if I unleash his feelings he may forget he is my father.

So. I'm riding home on the ferry. Sailing serenely into Neutral Bay. It's an ordinary everyday evening; if a dog barks in the distance I don't hear it, the terrain is too hilly for horses and if a messenger waits white-faced on the wharf, it's not to meet me. My head's full of my day's fun and labour, the way I've phrased a certain feeling to Frank; it's the phrasing, not the feeling, that's obsessing me – in fact this letter-writing stint has led me to the rather shocking conclusion that I'm prepared to sacrifice meaning to form. Any day. Even now. Writing this. So despite missing Frank, I think I could describe myself as happy in my struggle to find the perfect way to say so. I might even be humming a tune: an inconsequential old number from *Carousel*, 'What's the Use of Wund'ring', or some such. Certainly the noise of the engines shuddering into neutral and the crash of the gang-plank as the ferry ties up at the wharf are things that are happening outside my concentration: the climb up the steep hill home is automatic.

So it's strange when, automatically, I start to hurry. For some reason best known to themselves my legs start to move faster. And before I know it I'm running, and the effort is making me sweat, and the sweat is coming out cold, and freezing my heart. I'm in terror at what it is my body knows that I don't. The light is falling fast, dropping round my feet like soft scarves which I can't turn back and pick up because there isn't time. The postbox at the gate looks replete, but I don't stop to see if a letter's come, I rush on into the house, because the letter I'm envisaging now has no stamp on it, no address or blue airmail stickers, but comes in a plain white envelope with one ominous word on it: Rosalind. For my father always calls me by my proper name in moments of crisis, or sentiment.

And sure enough, there it is, propped up against the clock on the mantelpiece like any vulgar notice of abandonment. I rip it open, dreading its tone as much as I dread its content. But at this most terrible moment of my life, my father offers me a strange consolation: miraculously his letter doesn't embarrass me – I may turn deathly pale, but I don't turn red. In fact, of its genre, I find it exemplary.

This is how a suicide note sounds:

Tell the police I'm in my car, somewhere in French's Forest. Don't try to look for me yourself – it's too late to stop me now. I've posted a letter to my solicitor and one to your mother in England, telling them what I've done, so there's no going back.

I'm utterly broke, and the manner of my death will negate my life insurance, but the sale of my flat, bought in your mother's name for the purpose, ought to get you all out of immediate trouble.

There's enough cat food in the fridge to last five days. Also, a steak and kidney pie and some salad for your dinner. Not very exciting, I'm afraid, but I didn't have much time. Try to eat it anyway.

Love,
Dad.

There's a P.S. on a separate page.

That last was to show the police. This bit is only for you. You will be shocked and upset. Ring Adele [the marriage counsellor – number given]: she will be half expecting this. I know you don't like her much, but in the absence of your mother, she is kind, and will know what to do.

Take no notice of any demands for money – there is no need to pay anyone now that I am

dead except the painters to whom I promised
cash. You will find two hundred pounds in
notes under your pillow. Put it somewhere secret
and flush this letter, torn up, down the lavatory.

    I'm sorry to have done this to you, dearest girl,
of all people. But then you always knew you
were my favourite.

I flush more than the second half of the letter down
the loo. My stomach is not so much upset as suddenly
ultra efficient, as though evacuating itself urgently to
facilitate some major operation to come. And it's just as
well, for the panic that begins to run through my body
cuts as radically as any surgical knife. I don't know what
to do. I mean, I really don't know what to do on any
level: adjust my clothing, wash my hands, fall down in
a faint. I ask myself what would my mother do, and it
comes to me that whatever needed doing, she would
have done it already. She would have seen this coming
and not have let things come to such a pass. I have
failed her. It is worse, in a way, than having failed my
father.

For the want of an initiative of my own, I follow my
father's instructions, although I suspect I'm playing into
his hands, compounding his felony. I locate the two
hundred pounds under my pillow and stuff them into a
shoe under the bed, and then ring the police and read
them page one over the phone. They tell me not to
worry, people are often making these threats; he's
bound to walk through the door at any moment.
Instead of being comforted, I'm angry, I have my
father's dignity to think of. You don't know him, I start

shouting. He's tried this before. And failed, presumably, I hear the constable thinking, though to do him justice he manages to refrain from saying it. Has he been acting strangely at all? he comes up with instead.

Not particularly, I answer quickly, but I can tell from my voice, its sudden, closed dullness, that I'm lying. The truth is, my father has been acting very strangely indeed, even for him. For instance, just last night . . . But I can't think about that now. What shall I do? What shall I do? I start whimpering; and hysteria works with the policeman where self-control failed. Just stay where you are, dear, he says, and we'll send out a search party.

Ringing the counsellor is not so straightforward, as I've thrown her telephone number prematurely down the lavatory. But her practice is listed in the phone book, plus a likely home number at Balmoral Beach. As it's after hours I try the latter. A child answers and yells for her mother; when Adele comes on the line, her voice is all of a twitter. Why are you ringing me here? she says accusingly.

Well, you see, I say, it's just that Dad . . .

But in the absence of my mother, she is not kind. She has children of her own who need protecting. I'm afraid I know nothing about this, she says quickly, in a dull, closed voice. But if you'd like to consult me professionally, I'm available in office hours.

Shame on you, I say, although I know that the shame is on my father: on his taste, on his proclivities, on his poor clouded judgement. I put down the receiver, and with it all hope of help from his quarter. Who else can I ring? Not Nancy, whose father has just died naturally of an actual disease, or Jill whose father, the judge, might sit in judgement. I'm too new at university to have made any close friends – all the people I care about are in England. So in the end I dial the number of an old friend of my mother's, and almost before I've finished explaining, she's on the doorstep.

I'll never forget her. She wasn't someone I knew well, or have seen anything much of since: in fact she and I have since taken fairly strenuous pains to avoid each other, I suppose because the dreadful intensity of that night was not something that either of us cared to re-live. But that night she was kindness itself. Although unlikely casting for it. Like all my mother's friends she was a bit of an oddity, and quite unlike my mother. A tall, loud-voiced woman, slightly blowsy. Attractive really, although not – and this was crucial – my father's type. By which I mean she'd always made it clear she was rooting for my mother. More than that, she had theatrical connections, an anathema to my father: she'd been in amateur productions of plays my mother wrote before she was married, and my mother in her company became witty and slightly audacious, the girlish, talented person she had been in her youth. So you could say that this woman, whose name was Maude, had my father's number. And that when I rang her number that night, I took my mother's side for life.

Oh, but how comforting she was! She took my arm. She took the whole weight of my body and led me to the sofa where she sat me down and poured me a large glass of brandy. Then she made me a cup of tea to water it down. She fed the cat its allocated dinner, although she had less luck feeding me mine: solids were more than I could manage, so she ate my steak and kidney pie herself. Then, pointing out that I was still shaking, she tried to put me to bed; said we probably wouldn't hear anything till morning. But when my head touched the pillow under which the two hundred pounds had been hidden, I sprang up and said I must stay where I could hear the phone. And see the front door. After all, the police had said he was bound to walk in at any moment. So she dragged my mattress, unaided, into the hall. Lie down, she commanded, and lay down herself beside me.

It's a strange place, bed. It isn't just somewhere you go to sleep, or for sex, or when you're ill. Sometimes you just huddle there, curled up like a dog retreating to the basic territory of its basket. Like a dog I lay, guarding the telephone and the front door: the whole of my concentration was taken up with waiting. This woman, Maude, whom I hardly knew, lay fully clothed as I was, beside me. I was strangely unselfconscious in her company, on one level hardly aware of her; for although we drew close as humans do in times of extremity, she could only accompany me through the hours of darkness bodily, physically simulate, in her great tolerance and sympathy, the pattern I soon set up, wherein I would drift vaguely into blessed forgetful sleep, only to shake myself and her alert, because the moment that was worse than any knowledge, which threatened to dislodge my heart from its axis, was the moment of re-realization, of coming to the knowledge all over again, which happened every time between half-conscious-ness and waking. So although she kept vigil with my tossings and turnings and even followed me when I got up to have a pee, she couldn't follow my dreaming spirit into French's Forest, where with my goldilocks stuffed under my red riding hood I braved the wolves and bears that haunt the dark woods, in search of the gold-robed king who was my father, and found instead in a banal and foul-smelling Chevrolet a balding coward slumped over his own stilled horn. And better *that*, believe me, better *that* than the ghostly giant, the fee, fi, fo, fum monster whom the police had warned might come home at any moment; how I dreaded him now, how I feared the front door would open to admit my father in his resurrected state, staggering, unshaven, tears seeping from eyes that might never have seen me again, his lungs still sputtering fumes of carbon monoxide. I feared him. Fear was stronger in my nostrils than the smell of petrol. If he came home now, and started telling me in a slurred, broken voice he'd made a hash of it, I'd have to put my arms round him, however appalled I was, as a mother would a child. Or a daughter would a father. As I should have done last night.

For that is what my shame is: the night before he died I heard my father crying. I was out on the verandah in my pyjamas, breathing the wistaria-scented night air, in the middle of some half-phrased reverie to Frank . . . Do you remember, darling, how we . . . when above the whine of a mosquito that was plaguing me, I heard this sobbing. I hoped at first it was an animal in the garden, or at least some creature in his bedroom that my father was maltreating: it was such an embarrassing sound, such a terrible, unmanly, high-pitched, rhythmical whimpering that there could be no worse outcome in the world, than that it should be he, himself.

But it was. Through the falsetto yelping broke the occasional bass howl that was stifled so determinedly that a blubbering mechanism, almost amounting to a fit, would ensue. I believed then, as I almost believe now, that his overriding passion was that on no account should I be permitted to hear.

Should I have gone to him? It is the question that has hung over my life. His ghost tries to reassure me I should not: it has come back in many guises to reiterate that what a man needs most is his manhood, that what grief requires is simply to be left alone, and what a man values in a woman, as indeed a child does in a parent, is the quality, not of tenderness, but of discretion.

But I can't help wondering how it would have been if I'd been braver. Stepped over the arbitrary line that says that a daughter cannot be intimate with her father. If I'd listened to his secrets, told him his sins didn't matter, rocked him, as so many women had before me, against my breast, would I have saved him? Would he have thanked me? I only know that his fate was in my hands. And that there are fates, as we all know, worse than death.

So I went back to my newly painted bedroom. I shut the window, although the night was more than passing hot. I put cold cream on my face, wiped it off, brushed my teeth, killed a mosquito, read for a bit, turned off the light. And in the carelessness of my youth and health, I fell fast asleep.

I didn't go to him because I couldn't. And I couldn't because he was my father. We were alone there, you see. And I was afraid if he unleashed my feelings I might forget I was his child.

The police come at dawn. Maude's husband is with them, and a doctor. The mild way they tell me makes it sound like good news. We've found your father, is all they gravely say.

There is what scriptwriters call a beat, that strange hiatus between the cut and the appearance of the blood. And then grief comes over me like an admission, creeps into my pale anglicized skin like a blush. No one is fool enough to try to put their arms round me. I'm too busy to bear to be touched: the universe is readjusting itself rapidly around me like a theatrical set – the lights have gone out, trapdoors are flying open and a whole new landscape is dropping in from the flies. I'm alone on the stage.

And then a miracle happens. In front of this cross-section audience of plods and medics, the power of expression comes to me. And what I express is rage. Terrible sounds of fury start to emanate from my throat: I scream, I rail, I blaspheme against my father, or God, or whoever the fucker is who has been so stupid. My repertoire of expletives shrinks to an insistent shriek of *Why?* and I trample this one word into the mattress I've spent the night on, and throw myself face down and beat its brains out with my fists.

But the members of my audience aren't appreciative. My performance embarrasses them. They find it unseemly for a bereaved young woman to disport herself thus. Luckily there's a doctor in the house; he steps forward brandishing the needle he's brought along just in case; the two policemen grab me in mid-convulsion and hold me down. And I scream and kick to the last as they push up my skirt and pull down my pants and bare my bottom to administer grief's punishment.

The injection goes deep. The sedative works quickly. My cries are efficiently subdued, and with them all my violent love for my father, his helpless tallness, his thrilling temper, his wanton gallantry, it all goes underground, into a deep, drug-induced sleep from which no princess ever awakes for a hundred years. Well, twenty-five, in my case. But that's another story.

When I came round I was calm. So calm, I could feel nothing. Even for Frank. I stopped the letter I'd been writing to him in mid-sentence and posted no more. I interested myself in current college activities such as sleeping with the first shit who asked me. And the second shit as well. It made a change from poetry.

My mother flew back for the funeral, but I gave it a miss. I wasn't confident of the Church's position regarding suicide. I hitch-hiked to French's Forest and picked flowers there instead, and made myself dizzy breathing in their scent; but their fumes weren't lethal.

## 26

Frank fell in love with me on paper. Not that he hadn't wanted me in the flesh. But apparently my letters were what moved him. Moved him, that is, to dispense with his first wife. Luckily there were no children to deflect him from his purpose with any hackneyed ploys like stealing at school, coming out in spots or wetting the bed. It was just the woman he had versus the woman he didn't have. The usual fixed fight. What's more, the letters he loved me for had stopped. Without explanation. If I'd wanted to manipulate him I couldn't have done it more expertly. But we never learn, do we, because it's too sad a lesson: silence is all it takes.

Frank came to Australia to get me. Well – it wasn't his *sole* purpose – he'd wangled himself a commission to do some illustrations for a Poms' joke guide to the glories of Sydney Harbour. He turned up on the doorstep to surprise me. I was so surprised I wasn't there. My mother answered the door. She took one look at Frank, and with her usual faultless judgement, cool and clear in everything but the choice of her own husband, made up her mind he was for me. She asked him in, sat him on the verandah with my sisters, put on the first lipstick she'd worn since my father died, and made him quite a presentable cup of tea. So that when I got back from college, or, to put it more precisely, from the rather bug-ridden bed of a fellow student with whom I'd been spending a strenuously unliterary afternoon, there he was, already one of the family.

My overwhelming desire at the sight of him was to have a bath. I was furious, for one thing, and needed to cool down. It was two years since we'd seen each other, and nearly a year since we'd exchanged so much as a word. I wanted to wash away the taint of the time not spent together which clung to my skin like the unwholesome smell of a stranger. But you can't say just a minute to someone who's travelled twelve thousand miles to see you, even if you *have* travelled twelve thousand miles to get away from him. I shifted my glare to my mother, who in turn glared at my sisters, and the three of them had the sense to see that the plot would progress less stiffly if they vacated the verandah. And then my pleasure at having Frank here, so divinely out of context, had to be acknowledged; there was nothing I could do but go over to him and put my arms round him and kiss him, just as I was, with someone else's semen still inside me. Did he know? Could he tell? Roz, he said, Rosa, my Rose. And suddenly everything depended on the fact that he *did* know, knew but didn't care, wanted to embrace not just me, but all the stains and slurs and sorrows that had spoiled my life in the interim. Through our clothes I could feel his erection, cheerful and undiscriminating, as erections are, and because I was still at heart a perverse and depraved schoolgirl, and knew that my sense of pollution must give way soon enough to the sweet hygienic virtue of married love, I had a compulsion to have him now, in my mother's house, before time and soap and a more discreet venue could erode the originality of my sin.

I took him by the hand and led him silently through the hall to the bathroom; not that I was still intent on washing – far from it: it was simply the only room in the house with a reliable lock on the door. And no sooner had the bolt shot home than he was inside me, and the cool tiled floor was against my hot back; my self-disgust was overtaken by the pure delight I had always taken in him, and my stale juices were turned into life-giving balm; and sex, which (it being 1963) was supposed to have just begun, ended for me in the consecration of a hallowed rite.

We made things worse by falling asleep on the floor. He from jet-lag, I from the relaxation of a lifelong tension I hadn't even known I'd been subject to. One of my sisters, bursting for a pee, eventually had to bang on the door to wake us. But when we emerged there was a radiance about us that put us beyond the reach of disapproval. My mother didn't bat an eyelid. Lately she had come to think of me as my father's daughter, but in the matter of Frank I was all hers; she wanted him for me, and was prepared to go to certain lengths to get him: I caught her in the kitchen having a go at cleaning out the fridge. Perhaps she sensed the power in him not just to make me happy, but to bring me to the subjection she'd been brought to herself. Does he like roast lamb? she said. Do you want him to stay? He could sleep in your father's room if I can make enough space in the laundry to iron some sheets.

So Frank moved in. Although I made sure he spent most of his stay with us out and about. I didn't go back to college even to collect my books: we were too busy sailing back and forth across Sydney Harbour, from Hunter's Hill, to Taronga Zoo, to Luna Park. The Opera House was barely off the ground, but there were plenty of other landmarks for Frank to get his pencil around. Watching him draw, I looked at the sights as though for the first time, an ingenuous tourist in my own home town. He knew his limitations and didn't set out to capture the full sweep of the harbour: what you got with him were the barnacles on the jetties, the expressions on the faces of the seagulls. Bits of me stuck into his pictures, an elbow here, a hipbone there: the inevitable outcome of our always being pressed up against each other. Frank could only draw what he saw, and what he couldn't help looking at was me. Not that he would have dreamed of making a feature of me, any more than I would be prepared to describe him in any detail here: I was just the human factor, the dark bit in the foreground that ran through his sketches like a signature. He had the same attitude to drawing as I had to writing: that the personal, dwelt upon with enough fanaticism, will automatically give rise to the general.

He was certainly prolific in my company. And watching his profile silhouetted against some of Sydney's more vulgar sunsets, I felt the odd stanza rising to the surface myself. For two people to form a liaison that didn't naturally exclude the muse seemed to me an even rarer achievement than love. And there was another, more persuasive member of the wedding. After four months of sailing back and forth through ever more perfect weather and untroubled waters I started to feel uncharacteristically sea-sick. I'll look after you, said Frank, meaning both me and my unborn Mary. What could I say? They had me in their frank and foetal clutches. Oh, and I was so happy to be there. He went home to England to sort things out, and I flew to join him on my birthday. I was twenty-one years old, the Beatles were in the charts, and love really *is* all you need. And as the women's movement was rising, so I sank, singing, into a state of ecstatic dependence.

## 27

Edith swings on the gate. She runs down the garden path, jumps on to the wide-open gate and rides it until it clicks shut. I'm standing watching, on the doorstep, but I'm hardly in my body at all, so much of me is riding with her, straightening out from a crouched position to a stretched one and then swaying backwards to absorb the gate's sudden arrest, which she mimics in a tension at the backs of her knees, raised as she is with the wooden crossbar under the balls of her feet, her shoulders hunching and her neck retracting then growing long again as she leans over to wave goodbye to a friend. Edith is what you would call graceful. Meaning that an action like that, made up though it is of so many intricate adjustments – the run, the jump, the crouch, the stretch, the sway, the hunch, the lean, the wave – is somehow, when she does it, all of a piece, some perfectly predicted transition of the spirit from here to there, from open to shut, its last wave inherent in its first run. And inanimate things, like gates, respond as partners to her, taking her to their creaky, wooden embrace, lifting her lightness unfumblingly and setting it down, to some mysterious inner music of nature.

It's Edith's birthday. She's seven, or maybe six, or is it eight. Or perhaps I only think it was her birthday because that's all we're left with, the only record we keep of family life. Our albums and home movies are littered with them; the passing years are reduced to a recurring cake with candles and a bulging-eyed child, drawing in its hectic cheeks to blow. This gate-swinging sequence itself is recurrent; it seems to have replayed in my head over the years like the rushes of some tyrannical film director who has insisted on take after take even though the first one was plainly perfect; it's as though I'm trying to match these few brief frames of reality to some dream of childhood I had before Edith was born. Certainly she's dressed for a party, or is wearing fancy-dress or something glittery: Edith has a predilection for dressing up and totters about in my high heels and make-up; there are some hats of my mother's in an old trunk which are a source of fascination and hilarity to her; she parades their moth-eaten out-modedness with a startlingly precocious sense of chic. But by the time she starts her run down the path she's the worse for lemonade and sausage rolls – the dog has got her hat and is killing it and she's kicked off my patent leather slingbacks and hitched her trailing skirts into her knickers so that the waif in her is wild and unencumbered.

I watch with the joy of being more someone else than myself. I can allow myself this joy, which is love, because I am her mother; I am laying claim to the grace that transcends her inheritance from me. I turn and see Mary, nearly as tall as I am, standing just behind me, dressed, sportingly, as a waitress for her little sister's party. But her face, watching Edith, is the face of a mother: I recognize her expression as being exactly the same as my own. Doting. Speculative. The sort of look, which, when it's turned on her, tends to make her squirm. Why are you staring, Mum? she's likely to shout at me.

The answer is, I'm amazed. Amazed at the beauty and capriciousness of my children. The way they walk and talk and are so dazzling. Other people's children can do what they like, run too fast, lean over too far, I don't care. Oh, I'll catch them if I can, if I happen to be passing, I'll dive in, call an ambulance, soothe their grazed knees. But it won't be from passion. My passion is for my own entrails which walk the world as people with minds and hearts that are still half joined to mine. The passion I feel for my children exhausts me. It is making me old. It is what I will die from. And I've only felt its killing effects twice over: women used to have six, eight, ten, twelve children. Imagine all that passion under one roof, all that squirming, all those speculative looks. It's only taken two to teach me this one thing, that love can't be divided; it multiplies. My children see-saw in and out of my good books: when one rides high the other bounces muddily on the ground. But that's just a balancing act, a game, because they happen to be two. Or sometimes we form clubs: me with Mary, Frank with Edith, because we're four. But you don't value one child over another. You can't – it isn't possible, it isn't human. There was never a Choice as terrible as Sophie's. As a mother your stomach drops out at the obscenity of it. You'd rather die, leave your insides all over the floor, than have one part get up and exist at the expense of the other. Time, the great cake with candles,

147

has shamed me thus: there is not, there never could have been, a favourite.

## 28

I like to read books out of sequence. It's an indulgence I've always allowed myself, flipping them open at any old page and seeing where my eye becomes engaged. I place my trust in chance, rather than in the author's dubious intention, and good books, books worth reading, can be read endlessly by this method, since nothing need come to the last page that was not formally begun. It's not all laziness, or arrogance, it's just that, deprived of its system, fiction seems more like life to me: you come in anywhere and are privy to a lot of information you shouldn't be, while remaining ignorant of something essential, something intrinsic, upon which everything that comes before and after is based.

So that when my mother dies, and a huge bag of my father's letters to her falls into my clutches, those shuffled, unnumbered envelopes, rattling around in the depths of some grubby old canvas sack, into which I can reach as if into my own spider-ridden unconscious and see what I'm unlucky enough to draw out, seem to me to have all the components of fiction as I have known it: its empiricism, its randomness, its creeping boredom. I've sampled a few pages, and if it were a book it would certainly be one I'd read later rather than sooner. I don't like its tone, for a start. The tone, that is, that my father takes with my mother. Not that it isn't loving – in that sense it's extraordinary, revelatory: he writes to her with reverence and passion. What's more, the weight of his love for her is tangible, heavy to lift, takes up space, you keep tripping over it – there are *hundreds* and *hundreds* of letters in the bag. And the least of them is fourteen pages long. They make the paper I've covered to Frank seem pretty sparse. A short story in the face of a serious block-buster. Of course with this kind of output the repetitiveness of the message becomes a madness: I love you, I need you, begins to sound like some sort of tic. But it isn't the content that bothers me, it's the style. My father writes to my mother as though she were a baby. Belovedest. Little girl. My darling child. Or worse, he reverses roles and sits at her feet, calls her his madonna, and once, unabashedly, Mummy. Maybe it's just the romantic fashion of the day, but it makes me queasy. I stuff the letters back in the bag, tie a knot in the drawstring and have them shipped back in a crate from Australia, where I've had to go to attend my mother's funeral. I can't cope with everything at once. My mother's death is enough. I'm grateful to her for dying the ordinary way, the slow, humiliating, putrefying, natural way, for getting us used to her bones as we went along. But I need time to conceive of her as dust before I'm prepared to come across her restored to youth, in a hat that matches her eyes, in my father's letters. So when her effects arrive in England, although I prop up her framed photograph on my mantelpiece, I shove the sack into a damp corner of the cellar: with a bit of luck there'll be a flood, and his words will go soggy and run and be too blurry to read, with or without my glasses.

But by the time my courage comes back, the bag has disappeared. It must have been given to Oxfam or gnawed by mice or thrown out on a skip. And suddenly I'm desperate, I'm a forty-five-year-old orphan and those letters are the fabric of my life: I start clutching my head and moaning, Where have they gone? Frank, who's more methodical than I am, sorts through all our junk meticulously, but he can't find them either. They've been spirited away.

Or upstairs at least. For one day Edith comes into my study, tall and strong enough now to carry single-handed a full black plastic dustbin liner which she dumps at my feet. Do these, she asks, have something to do with you? I found them in an old sack in the attic which was made of canvas. I hope you don't mind but I've cut the stuff up into pieces. I thought if I stretched it I might be able to use it to paint on.

Far be it from me to come between an artist and her material. Besides, Edith has done me a service in tipping the letters from one bag to another; the earliest ones, which were at the bottom, are now on top. They've fallen into chronological order: I'm being forced to open the book at chapter one.

Here, then, is my father when he first met my mother. And now there's no sentimental patronization, no little boy blues. All that was just sublimated sex in an age when men had to pretend to women that all they really wanted to do was snuggle up to them. *Rest* in their arms. As though people in their twenties were always *tired*. Here, before he knows her, he woos her in language that is stilted and decorous, like the language of the law. And indeed his office address proclaims a firm of barristers. There is talk of acting for people. Getting costs. My father was a lawyer! What is your father? people used to say to me. I never really knew how to answer. The question always made me uneasy, as though it struck at something deeper than an idle interest in how my father happened to make his living. He runs a business, I would say, that advises other businesses how to run their affairs. But the answer never really made sense to me. Not just because my father's own affairs were always in such disarray. I was answering the wrong question. I was saying what he *did* because I had no idea what he was. He was certainly not what he seemed. In the rough and ready Sydney of the fifties, men like my father, tall, charismatic, educated men with beautiful handwriting, could be anything they liked. A doctor, a farmer, a politician: it was a matter of vocation. And yet my father had none. Nor had he been to war, as nearly all my friends' fathers had. Much emphasis was laid on his sciatica, and I did see him crippled with it once. But it didn't explain the blank at the centre of his life, the sense of the vital pages of the book of him having been stuck together or flipped over or ripped out from the spine.

And now I'm holding those missing pages in my hand. Oh, I don't mean the ones that prove that he did, after all, have a profession, or even the ones containing certain astonishing references to a first wife, whom neither he nor my mother ever mentioned. Those are just twists in the plot, due as much to the questions I never bothered to ask as to my parents' propensity for secrecy. No, the pages I'm talking about make my hands shake to hold them. They jump-start my heart, and turn my cheeks dull red. They come from an envelope fifty letters deep, after my father had known my mother for about a year. There's a strange blue mark across the left-hand corner of the envelope, which at first I don't take into account. They're written on long, cheap, yellowing, ruled paper, so different from his usual watermarked vellum; the word this paper makes me think of is institutional. And my father's lavish handwriting has gone small. It's shrunk to a third of its size. It's trying to conserve space, as though there's too much to say and not enough paper to say it on. Or it's trying to hide itself. It's afraid of being read. It's cowering from the sight of eyes that are not my mother's. And the tone is weird: self-conscious, unforthcoming, coded. No more darlings or beloveds: Dear cousin. But they're not related. There's the same blue mark across the corner of each page as there was on the envelope. It's only made by a small rubber stamp, but it stamps out freedom. It is the mark of a censor.

My father went to prison.

It's so simple when you know it, it can be said in one short sentence, the one that sentenced my father to two years. The crime scarcely matters to me here. Oh, I could make out a case for his innocence of whatever it was he was accused of, which, if his garbled explanations to my mother are anything to go by, had to do with a milk company, a vengeful mistress and some shares which he rashly underwrote. Clearly he was made a scapegoat by the law society, which turned on him as such establishments do turn on their own. But between the shares and the milk and the woman, I expect he was guilty. Guilty of an essential profligacy of nature, of raising his hat to one bitch or shit too many. More, I suspect him of being relieved to have been locked away. Behind bars, a strange calm seems to have come over him. Hard labour affects him beneficially, like rest. The gruel he's given to eat, the sackcloth he's given to sleep on don't bother him. He catalogues the gruesome privations of the place with the wry acceptance of a boarder writing home from school. Some innate fear has left him: the fear of what terrible conflagration he might set off next. He's been reprieved from the responsibility of his own mad optimism; he's flown too high, hit his head on the rafters, and now finds an unexpected support on the cold stone floor. There's no currency here except cigarettes, and since he doesn't smoke, he's rich in the privileges he wants, such as pen and paper. There are no women either: all he has is the photograph of my mother that he's smuggled into his cell inside a book. Her gaze is gentle and steadfast: she's the only one he cares about; if it weren't for her he wouldn't care what became of him.

My father's true favourite was my mother. His failure, his fallibility, the highest treasures of his soul are piled up in these letters at her feet. All I ever wanted as a child was that this should be so. And now that I find it is, I feel shocked and betrayed. He trusted her – why could he not trust *me*? Did he think me less steadfast, less gentle? I suppose if he'd been made bankrupt, his record would have come out in court: did he think I would take the judge's daughter's side against him? Did he die rather than let us discover his secret? When that discovery alone could have set his children free from the feeling that they were somehow to blame?

I used to have a persistent dream in which my father and I were high up on a mountain. We had run away as far as we could, and now there were people on all sides climbing after us. My father had done something dreadful: there was blood all over his hands and a wild, hunted look in his eyes. I wasn't afraid of him. I was in an agony of compassion for him, it was my job to stay with him, to hide him, if I could, under a rock. The dream wasn't a nightmare: what I remember is exhilaration at being up so high, and breathing such cool, clean air, and knowing with such fierce purpose what I must do.

I'll never be able to dream that dream again. You'd be a bit embarrassed, wouldn't you, even in your sleep, if the murderer you were shielding turned out to be, at worst, a petty embezzler. My father went to prison. His sentence sets me free. The shackles fall from me, the iron door swings open, I can see sky. So why am I crying? Is it for my mother who has, after all, only just died? Her soft gaze in the photo on my mantelpiece hardens perceptibly. Was it her blood I saw on his hands in my dream? They talk a lot these days about the lust men feel for their daughters. But they forget the nature of a little girl's love for her father.

Its bright innocence.

Its dark passion.

## 29

Mary plays the cello. When we moved back to town she had to give up riding, and the huge, gleaming brown instrument that her new school was open-handed enough to lend her seemed at first just to be filling the empty gap in her affections, not to mention between her knees. The noise it made when she sat astride it was like the complaint of an ill-used animal, and we pitied the poor school orchestra that had to ride out the duration of her obsession.

But the obsession didn't go away. She surprised Frank and me by bringing the instrument to her will. And now, after fifteen years, the throbbing response her practised embrace draws from it seems to be happening in our own veins as she carries us with her through sonorous inner landscapes with the wind in our hair. The effort to produce the music is so physical that it makes her shake involuntarily as though with a palsy, and her fingers strum themselves into such a masturbatory frenzy that we are sometimes ashamed of the voyeurism involved in watching her, not least because of the transport in her face which is full of a flushing, naked, unmasked candour, the same expression that I sometimes catch on Edith's face when she's painting. The same expression, come to that, I once caught on my own face, when my first lover, Alfred's successor, the one I *did* sleep with, pushed me up off the bed and before him towards the wardrobe mirror where, looming over and around me, pressed hard up behind me, gripping my upper arms, he cried, Look at your face, how it looks when I'm inside you: *look*! And I saw my face, most itself in the service of a passion.

Watch! Mary used to beg us, when she thought she was a horse. Now that we know she's a cello, we can't take our eyes off her. Nor can the young men who fall prey to the beauty that seems to emanate from the power in her trained, bared shoulders. We call her suitors her swains: it's our way of keeping them in their places. All the swains have square jaws and come armed with bunches of roses. When I say all, I mean four. I mean one after the other. But they have a corporate image. They have all loped down to the bathroom in their day in the same towelling dressing gown of Mary's. They have all made deep friends with the dog, and been welcomed by him passionately long after their reception from Mary has cooled off. Their lean, sporty, well set-up young bodies have all developed the same slight limp of exhaustion as though they've been expected to scale the wall of too high a tower, or hack their way through too many brambles. For the truth is, Mary refuses to be won. Now a woman in her middle twenties, she wants to stay locked up in the enchanted castle of the happy childhood which we did, after all, manage to give her. Oh, she *sleeps* with her young men, condoms permitting, in this death-by-sex era. She brings them home to stay the night as though they were schoolfriends (she did go to school with one of them, as it happens). But she doesn't go and live with them at their places. She likes it here, with the washing machine and us. So too, to do them justice, do the swains. The sons of schoolmasters and brigadiers who told them to sit up straight and watch their language, they like to sprawl with us round our kitchen table, watching Mary and Edith telling their father to fuck off to his face. The swains draw in their breath audibly for the ensuing explosion, but none comes. If Frank loses his temper, and he often does, it will be at something political he's read in the morning papers. As for me, I'm laughing: nothing could make me more happy or more proud than the proof that my girls are not afraid of their father.

But when the novelty wears off, the swains get restless. However high-spirited the fair maiden, how can they save her if the dragon refuses to breathe fire? For we are subtle ogres, we liberal parents. We come in the guise of irreplaceable friends.

It's not until one of the Bach Unaccompanied Suites starts to reverberate from the music room, a sure sign that the resident companion is on the way out, that I start to see the swain in his own right, distinct from the others. For unhappiness fosters originality, even if it's just in the hour a person chooses to invoke the answerphone and then not speak, or in what condition of car or plimsoll he lurks outside the house. Their apostolic names, Matthew, Mark, Luke, play tricks with your tongue and slip out instead of the name of the present incumbent. And when you see them again (Mary always stays friends with them for ever) you're peculiarly moved, as though they meant something to you quite apart from your daughter. Perhaps it has to do with having no sons or brothers that I miss them as much as I do when they're gone. They're all so tall, you see. Some taller than others. Bluer eyed. Fonder of the dog.

Fondest of all is Fred. Short for Frederick, not Alfred, although his hair does grow low on his forehead. He's the only person now who calls me by my full name, Rosalind, and for some reason it does give him special status with me. He wears his hair schoolboy short, but with a lock at the front which flops down over his eyes, and he has a way of looking out from under it that would produce a catch in any mother's throat. Actually, he's old, as surrogate sons go: midway, if the truth be known, between my age and Mary's. An older man, in *her* eyes, which got him nowhere; she doesn't intend to follow in my footsteps. Nearly two years after they've separated he's still coming back to the house on the off-chance that she's changed her mind and wants him back.

She's rehearsing, I lie. In Madrid, I add, in case he's thinking of turning up at one of her concerts. The truth is I don't have the faintest idea where she is. I can't tell him she's met a composer who's made *her* cry for a change, with the result that she's moved all her hi-fi equipment to his place.

Fred comes in anyway, he's brought a ball for the dog (a younger, smaller version of our old, now dead, one). Fred's shirtsleeves are rolled back to the elbow to facilitate his lovely overarm pitch; the dog rushes to the bottom of the garden to receive. Fred throws, the dog fetches, they are tireless, man and beast; I don't know why it makes me so happy to watch them.

I bring some whisky and water out on to the terrace. I know what Fred likes: after all, he used to live here. We're easy, Fred and I, we have a lot in common, such as missing Mary dreadfully, for a start. Fred wants to be a poet, although he's stuck at the moment in advertising, reduced to writing jingles for the Milk Board. He's brilliant at crosswords: when the family played Dirty Scrabble he outdid even Edith as champion of filth. But he was a strange boy, moody and withdrawn in the face of Mary's extrovert, hoydenish warmth: Frank and I were relieved when their affair proved short lived. Despite his beauty, he couldn't have been less eligible, and he led her quite a dance in his heart-breaking way. He suffers from phobias: claustrophobia, agoraphobia, and once a bout of kleptomania that involved the police. He's just packed in his job, and says he can't bear to see anyone; I have to remind him gently he's seeing me. Then I remember that seeing is the euphemism the young use these days for fucking, or having a relationship, or whatever it is they do – by Edith's rules, seeing could gain you seven points, plus land you a triple word score if you happened to be her. But with no Scrabble board in front of me, I blush to a blotchy red on my neck and chest as well as my face: these hot flushes they talk about are only the outcome of a new kind of embarrassment, a withering, not of the ovaries, but of the ego. I'm forty-seven years of age, he must think I'm as old as God, so what is this shyness that strikes me as though I were a girl? Fred's moody glance has lighted on me, I'm convinced he favours me in some way, that of all the people in the world, I am one he can bear. I start squinting and shading my eyes with my hand, although, to tell the truth, the evening sun is weak. Let's go inside, I say, and hurry on ahead, calling out to Frank to come down from his studio to join us.

But the next time Fred drops in, Frank's not in the house. It's not exactly an accident: Fred rang and asked when he could come, and actually it took some organizing for me to be here alone, since Frank and I are hardly ever out of the sight of each other; it's our way now, as in the old days, to do everything together. But at my suggestion, he and Edith have gone off to the Tate. I warned Fred they wouldn't be here, that Mary was still on tour, but he said it didn't matter. Apparently he wants to show me some of his poetry.

I cook what I remember him liking: spinach soup. It tastes pretty bilious in the light of the poems, which, if I am any judge, are the work of a madman, full of terrifying images of dismemberment: I'm more relieved than ever that Mary has escaped him. I'm used to peeling fruit and passing it round to my whole family, so when he quarters a pear for me and tenderly cuts the core out, I can't help finding his action disproportionately gallant. The flowers he's brought are on the table between us: white daisies. But he talks in one of his poems of eating the heads off just such ingenuous blooms and spewing them up. Nevertheless there's something about him that moves me, that I delight in: a sweet eagerness in his face that belies the poisoned cynicism of his pen. By the time we get up from the table we've had rather more wine than soup: the urge to touch him is so motherly it's almost natural. But I hardly need add that at my late stage of life you have to keep such feelings strictly to yourself.

We can't go into the garden today, it's raining. Fred sprawls in what is usually Frank's chair, while the dog plants the odd hopeful tennis ball in his lap. He's telling me his troubles. I've long since realized they're rather more elaborate than the incidental loss of Mary. He didn't pack his job in, apparently: he was sacked. He was accused, falsely, he claims, of appropriating company funds. If they prosecute he'll almost certainly face a gaol sentence. His shoplifting spree will be dug up in evidence against him. It isn't that he gives a shit what becomes of him, he hopes I understand. But he's afraid of the confinement, the physical proximity of all those inmates.

And all the time he's telling me these things, he's smiling. Some people pour out their troubles whether you want to hear them or not. But Fred offers his diffidently, like gifts. He gets up, dislodging the ball, which rolls in slow motion across the floor, but the dog knows that this is not a game. Fred's considering me, wondering whether I'm worthy of further confidence: he leans an elbow idly on the mantelpiece, slightly unsettling the propped-up portrait of my mother. He looks down, he's shy, his eyelashes sweep his cheeks as though what he is about to impart is a piece of coquetry, a girlish and beguiling secret. You see, he says, I'm afraid . . .

Afraid of what? I ask.

And then he says it, the thing that makes me get to my feet, brave my mother's stare, cross the room, step over the line, run the risk, start my life all over again;

162

take him in my arms as I should have done, Daddy, I
should have done:

I'm afraid I'm going to kill myself, he says.